HALF CRIME

Rusty Barnes

Acknowledgments

Thanks to: Eric Beetner, David McNamara, S.A. Cosby, Nikki Dolson, Paul J. Garth, Valerie Macewan, JM Taylor, Gabriel Valjan, Scott Von Doviak, Steve Weddle, and to the Discord crew. Thanks to the editors who previously published some of these stories, albeit in different form: April Michele Bratten, Up the Staircase Quarterly; David Cranmer, BEAT to a PULP; Paul J. Garth, Rock & a Hard Place; Joseph D. Haske, Sleipnir; David James Keaton, Dirty Boulevard; John Molina, Goliad Review; Ron Earl Phillips, Shotgun Honey Recoil.

Redneck Press
119 Bradstreet Avenue
Revere, MA 02151

ISBN: 979-8-218-25890-0 (paperback)
ISBN: 979-8-218-25891-7 (e-book)

Cover Design: Eric Beetner
Interior: David McNamara / Publish Publish

PRAISE FOR HALF CRIME

"The characters in this collection have been brought low by circumstances or their own actions, but Rusty Barnes is clear-eyed and compassionate in telling their stories, which can be grisly or heartbreaking or—most often—both at the same time."

—Scott Von Doviak, author of *Lowdown Road*

"A writer of incredible humanity, Rusty Barnes doesn't just know the blood that beats through the heart, he knows how it spills as well. Beautiful, poignant, and muscular, *Half Crime* is a collection that doesn't look away, and promises something special to both readers who refuse to flinch, and those who feel with everything they have."

—Paul J. Garth, author of *The Low White Plain*

"Tender and tough, these short stories in *Half Crime* from Rusty Barnes will remind you of the hardscrabble, hard-drinking, and hard-living characters from Andre Dubus; they're desperate but dignified, and they can't do wrong right. With a poet's eye for imagery and a turn of phrase, Rusty Barnes is a writer who deserves more attention and readers. *Half Crime* is all that."

—Gabriel Valjan, Agatha-, Anthony-, and Shamus-nominated author of the Shane Cleary Mystery series

"From Chimney Hill Road to Drag Hill, the settings in Rusty Barnes's *Half Crime* are as alive as the characters, who struggle through their lives among box cutters and knife fights, broken bones and busted dreams. Beautiful and brutal, *Half Crime* will appeal to fans of Daniel Woodrell and Tim Gautreaux."

—Steve Weddle, author of Country Hardball

"In each story of *Half Crime*, Rusty Barnes creates an entire world like a jewel—small and hard and beautiful. He brings the desperation of his rural characters to life with poetic empathy and simmering violence. Broken by poverty or pain, or just bad luck, they bring the reader with them on unforgiving journeys to find just a nugget of solace or compassion. Barnes is a deft and uncompromising writer who can reveal the beauty in even the most heartbreaking circumstances.

—J.M. Taylor, author of
Night of the Furies and Dark Heat

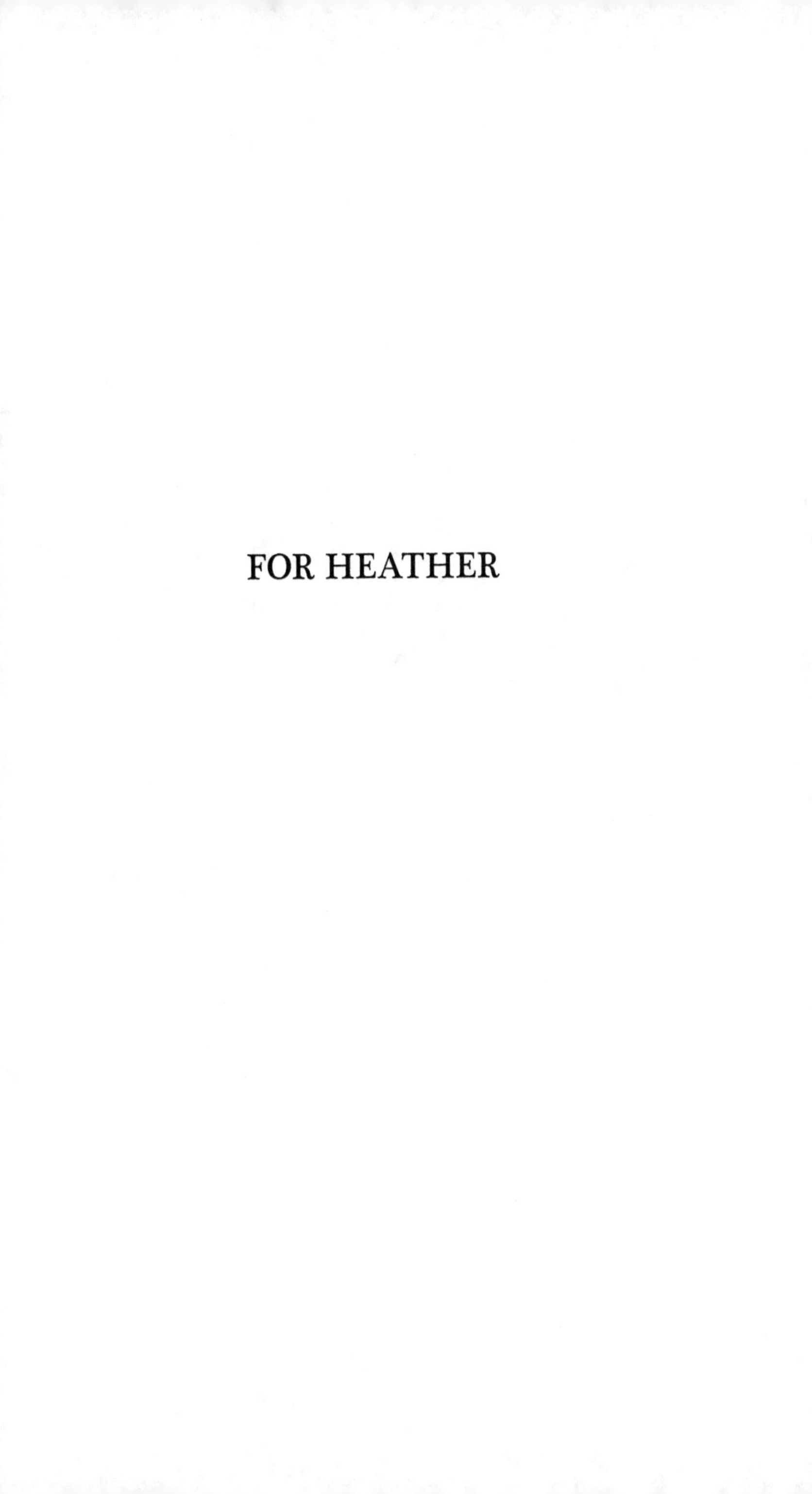

FOR HEATHER

TABLE OF CONTENTS

BAD OLD BOY

Crate Lang took a heavy blow against his chin, feeling the ring on Robbie Moore's finger crack against the dimple his wife loved, sending a dull ache into his entire jaw. Robbie pulled his fist back and circled around Crate like a boxer, hands up in front of his own face, glowering like a cartoon bulldog. Crate had a habit of fucking up.

"I told you," Robbie said. "You fuck with me, you pay." Crate crouched into his own stance and then thought better of it. What possible good could this do?

"Fuck it," Crate said, straightening. He offered his open hands to Robbie. "You're right. I fucked with the wrong man. You're a good ole boy, Robbie, and I don't want to fight you. Here—" Crate held up one hand, palm out, and reached for his wallet with the other." I owe you a hundred bucks. Take one twenty-five."

"It's worth three hundred," Robbie said uneasily. "My brother Dexter said you were a straight shooter."

"But we agreed on a hundred. I'm giving you a buck and a quarter." Crate held out his wallet and shook it.

"That pup is a gold mine," Robbie said.

"You didn't pay a red cent for that pup and it's never treed a coon," Crate said. "I'm giving you a deal. My kid needs a pup even if it won't tree."

"I still feel like you're ripping me off," Robbie said, and held out his hand. Crate counted out six twenties and five ones.

"And you got me one on the jaw," Crate said. "I'll forgive that little forget-me-not." All around them the crowd of men dispersed, murmuring. The small group of farmers and 4-H leaders went back to the tractor pulls in front of the grandstand, and Crate sighed with relief. The pup was wormy and poor, but his grandsire had been a hell of a dog, and he hoped the blood would tell. And if it didn't, even then, little Jefferson would crow over it, and Jeanelle would have to make the best of it, as she so often did with Crate.

* * *

Crate drove his Ford Escort back over Chimney Hollow Road with the dog in the passenger seat, keeping between the ditches and swerving occasionally for potholes, the dust swirling up into his open window. He'd opened a bottle of water and left it in the cupholder, and already the mouth of it tasted like dirt.

Jeanelle would have dinner ready by now, and Jefferson would be sitting in his high chair with a plastic bowl full of Cheerios and his sippy cup. Crate sighed. He'd worked from 4 a.m. to 4 p.m. before stopping to see Robbie Moore about the dog. "Gonna call you Butch," Crate said, scratching the pup behind its ears. The pup licked his jowls. "I know. I'm hungry too."

The road bottomed out near a farm pond surrounded by white fence, a couple ducks swimming on its surface. Crate saw the trailer laid out on the other side of the road, skirting piled hip-high by the front door. He'd hoped to put it on this past weekend, but Jeanelle's mother, Sarah, and her boyfriend, Cal, showed up and five bottles of wine later he didn't feel like putting it up.

Jeanelle pitched a little fit about it, but smiled thinly as Sarah and Cal drove off, Jefferson squalling on her hip. She'd spoken to Crate only briefly since then, and he hoped to make it up to her with the pup, but he was half-certain she wouldn't believe he'd gotten the boy a coonhound, even though he'd extolled the virtues of boy and dog many times before.

Pulling into the front yard, he hit the brakes slightly as he drove over the drainpipe and parked next to Jeanelle's truck. He gathered the pup in one hand and the worming medicine in the other and went into the trailer. The trailer smelled of fried chicken, and a slight mist gathered around the globe of light in the kitchen. Jeanelle had put on lipstick, which was unusual during the day, and she'd changed Jefferson into a clean onesie for dinner. The boy battered his cup against the plastic chair, chanting, "Da-DA, Da-DA, Da-DA," which made Crate feel pretty good, all things considered.

"Look what I got for you," Crate said, putting Butch up to the boy's face. Jefferson sniffed once and grabbed the dog by the ears. "Da-DA," he said.

"Yep, it's me. This here's Butch," Crate said. Jeanelle came around the table and touched the dog on the head.

"It's a nice dog," Jeanelle said. "I just wish you'd told me first." She took the dog down and drew some water in a margarine bowl and tucked it near the garbage can, where Butch began slopping it.

"I had an opportunity," Crate said. "I just couldn't pass it up."

"What happened to your face?" Jeanelle said.

"Nothing," Crate said. "Met up with a wrench. Bruised me a little."

"Uh-huh," Jeanelle said, her eyes half-lidded. "Dinner's on." Crate sat down at the table next to Jefferson and fed him applesauce from his own spoon. "So how was work?" Jeanelle kept asking him how work was going, but it didn't change much from day to day. Still new at the job, Crate spent a lot of days on top of a machine breaking rocks too large to go through the hopper, then at the end of the day helping the regular drivers grease the loaders and doing whatever else came up for the man on the lowest end of the seniority list.

"It was fine. Busted rocks, helped Ricky adjust the belts thirty feet up in the air." Crate pulled a piece of chicken out from his teeth.

"A little dangerous." Jeanelle toyed with the food on her plate. "I worry about you crawling around on top of the plant."

"No worries, babe," Crate said. "It's just that every-body has to do it. Eventually somebody else will be the low man and I'll be doing something else. The pay is great." He tried to change the subject. "How was your day?"

Jeanelle took a sip of her iced tea. "It's fine. Mom called. She and Cal picked up a new washing machine from the Deckers. It's mostly new. Sheila Decker just decided she wanted a new one so they sold it off for cheap."

"That's good," Crate said. "This chicken is fanfuck-ingtastic."

"Creighton. Why are we talking about the chicken?" Jeanelle folded her hands under her chin.

"What?"

"You didn't get that bruise from a wrench. I can see the mark of a knuckle or something."

"It's nothing, Jean. I had a disagreement with Robbie Moore, Dexter's brother. About the dog."

"So he hit you."

"He wanted more money than I was willing to pay."

"So he hit you?"

"I wanted the dog. We agreed on a price, then it wasn't what he wanted. I paid him a little more."

"How much more?" Jeanelle said.

"Just twenty-five bucks."

"How much did you pay for the dog?" Jeanelle sat back in her chair.

"Not much."

"We need that money," Jeanelle said. "The baby's doctor bill is due soon, and we haven't paid off my hysterectomy yet. I understand you wanted a dog for Jeff, but it's just not good right now."

"I'll get some money," Crate said. "Maybe I can pick up a little more overtime."

"You're working sixty hours a week already. You're going to fucking kill yourself." Jeanelle's eyes rose in tears.

"What choice do we have?" Crate said. "I just wanted a dog. The doctors can wait another month. Jeff's only going to be young once."

"He's only a little over a year old."

"It's important to start him out right. I didn't get a dog until I was five and I was already scared of them. I want Jeff to grow up with one, so he's not scared. I don't want him scared." Crate straightened his back and put his fork down. "I'm not hungry anymore."

"Crate. Don't do this."

"I've got a little daylight left. I'm going to hang that skirting around the front, so we don't look like white trash." Crate's chair banged back against the molding as he rose. It was 6:30. He had maybe two or three hours of daylight left, and a load of anger with no place to put it.

*　*　*

Crate hauled a square of skirting up and leaned it

against the trailer. He picked up a bottle of beer and drained half of it. Hipster beer, but he liked it. Fuck it. "Jeanelle," he called in through the screen door. "Get Jeff around. We're going to get ice cream." Inside the trailer he heard Jeanelle say something indistinct, and Jefferson's babbling reached a high pitch, then relaxed again like a bubble bursting. Ice cream would be a good thing, something to get his mind off his money trouble and onto something other than the troubled expression he'd seen on Jeanelle's face. It would take the last twenty dollars in his wallet, but it'd be good for everyone. Jeff would make a mess that Crate could clean up with baby wipes and get back on Jeanelle's good side, and later on in the dark while Jeff slept they could move together.

Jeanelle came to the door and poked her head out. "You're sure? Four is going to come awful early."

"I need to get out. You need to get out."

"I'm not going to lie. A hot fudge sundae would go down sweet." Jeanelle's head disappeared, and Crate picked up his T-shirt and put it back on, tucking the hammer and box of nails under the trailer. He stopped by the back of the trailer and washed his hands and face under the outside spigot. He considered his options. He could work overtime, provided the opportunity presented itself. He could cut wood on weekend nights and sell it this fall. He could get another job, but he needed something quicker than that, something that would quiet Jeanelle's worries and provide for Jefferson. He wondered if his mother-in-law's boyfriend needed any extra help. Cal installed security systems for the newly gas-rich farmers who suddenly had more money than they'd ever had before and wanted to protect their assets. Eventually that business would slow, but right now a lot of well-off farmers had bought expensive guns and entertainment systems, and needed protection from the itinerant gas industry workers who'd been shipped in from all over the country as well as the local tweakers. He could talk to Cal about that tomorrow after work.

Jeanelle came out with Jeff on one hip, locking the trailer door behind her. Crate jumped in on the passenger side of her truck, fastened Jeff into his car seat and the dog sat on the floor next to his feet. Jeanelle adjusted her side mirror and they left, bumping over the drainage ditch and down the dirt road to Coryland Road and eventually toward the Fair Shake. The country sat in full bloom around them, the fields heavy with hay and oats and the green trees beyond, still full of middle-growth trees and large patches of evergreen. Crate and Dexter had been out last week spotting deer and counted sixty-five before they got bored and started back for home. The black bears were out in abundance, and except for the frackers and the passingly curious fact that there were still very few jobs, the place was ideal for an outdoors-oriented family.

The blacktop road ran before them bright and shiny, one of the fringe benefits from the natural gas industry. All those trucks running back and forth needed good roads, and they roared down the hill at sixty-five miles an hour just because they could, singing along to country songs on the radio. They crossed into New York and slowed the truck before turning left into Pine City. The Fair Shake did a banging business during the summer, even though the sundaes had gotten more expensive like everything else. People liked to sit at their picnic tables and eat their butter pecan ice cream in peace, gossiping with the neighbors they knew they'd find there.

Jeanelle walked up to the window with Crate's wallet in her hand and ordered while Crate and Jeff sat at a table and waited for her. She came back first with her sundae and Jeff's baby cone, then went back to pick up Crate's vanilla malt. Tonight they had the place nearly to themselves. Another couple and their small children gathered around the goldfish pond with their cones and a larger group had gathered near the rear, talking loudly and ordering multiple large sundaes to share. Soon he saw his good friend Dexter Moore pull up with his girlfriend, Caitlin, and he left Jeanelle talking with a friend of her mother's and went over to talk with Dexter.

"Hey, Dex," Crate said.

"I hear you tangled with Robbie today." Dexter Moore stood about six feet tall and maybe a hundred thirty pounds of wire and muscle in a green T-shirt. He worked for the cable company as an installer and always seemed to have a finger in moneymaking schemes. He'd never involved Crate, but Crate trusted him, and he thought quickly about his current situation and decided what the hell. He'd see what his friend had to offer.

"Wasn't much of a tangle. He got his money," Crate said, dangling his milkshake from one hand.

"Sorry about that. Robbie's a pushy sonofabitch." Caitlin sighed dramatically and left Dexter to go talk with Jeanelle.

"I know it now. Hey, man," Crate lowered his voice so Jeanelle couldn't hear. "I need to make some quick cash. You know of anyone hiring or anything I could get into?"

"I don't know, man," Dexter said. "How bad off are you?"

"Oh you know. Bills and stuff. I just can't get ahead. I could use a couple extra checks."

"Couldn't we all?" Dexter said. "I don't know, man."

"Come on. You must know something. I know you're never hurting for money. You've always got extra."

"I can float you a couple hundred right now if you need it," Dexter said.

"Nope. I don't want to borrow. I want to make."

Dexter lowered his voice to a whisper. "If you can keep it quiet, I know a way you can make an easy grand. You have to come through though, because I'd be letting you in on it with these guys who don't like changes. I'm flush right now, but you can do the thing. It's basically just making a run into Syracuse and coming back. Easy-peasy. You show up, hand them the package, they hand you money. Cash and carry. Once every month. By December, all your money problems could be solved. It ain't exactly aboveboard, though."

Crate thought of Jeanelle. Jefferson. More overtime. Never being able to get ahead. Just then the dog ran

over to him, followed by Jefferson squealing and tod-
dling his way over. "That's OK," Crate said. "I'm in."

* * *

Later that night, Jeanelle straddled him on the bed
while Jefferson slept in the crib on the other side of
the room. Crate was distracted and even though he
performed all right his mind kept running off in different directions like a dog catching all the scents at
once. Jeanelle finished but he didn't, and she tumbled
off him in a heap and tucked herself into his arm.
"Sorry, baby," Crate said, cradling her breast in his
hand.

"I'm sorry I got on you about the dog. It'll be a good
thing." Jeanelle toyed with his chest hair.

"Yeah, Jeff sure likes him."

"Did you see the way he ran in the parking lot? Those
little stumpy legs."

"Hey, Jeanelle." Crate turned toward her. "I think I'm
going to call Cal in the morning on the way to work,
see if he has anything I can do on weekends. Get some
money to get ahead a little."

"I don't know. Maybe that would work. He doesn't
have anybody helping him anymore, but he'll probably need more hours than you can give."

"Maybe this winter then. After I get laid off."

"It'd be nice not to have to rely on unemployment this
winter." Jeff squalled a little in his sleep, and Jeanelle
got out of bed to soothe him with a bottle.

"I got a feeling everything's going to work out," Crate said, even though he was unsure. Jeanelle needed to hear it.

* * *

The next morning on the way in to work Crate left a message on Cal's cell phone. Cal called him back on his way home.

"You need money, son?" Cal's voice was hard and angular in Crate's ear, but he knew he meant well.

"Everybody needs money, Cal."

"I don't have nothing for you on weekends. Most of my work is done in the week. Only once in a while these rich rednecks want me to come in and rewire their houses then. They want the weekends for fun."

"I thought it was worth the effort. Thanks, Cal. How's Sarah?"

"She's a mean old lady just like always." Cal laughed. Crate laughed back at him and pressed off the phone. He'd just turned on the radio when his phone buzzed again, this time with a text from Dexter: *they want the delivery tonight. u ready?*

Crate pulled the car off to the side of the road and texted him back. The phone buzzed again almost immediately with an address near Syracuse: LaFayette, New York. He'd have to fill the tank before he left. It was 4:15. He texted Jeanelle and told her he'd be home really late. He blamed it on Dexter needing help, as he sometimes did. Jeanelle wouldn't think it too much out of the ordinary. Crate felt a surge of adrenaline come over him. He drove to Dexter's house to pick up. Dexter waited outside, smoking a cigarette, a smaller package than Crate expected clutched tightly in his right hand.

"Hey, man," Crate said. Dexter handed him the package.

"You ready for this?" Dexter said.

"Ready for what? Just a delivery. In and out. Like delivering a pizza." Crate knew it was more than that. He just didn't want to admit his nerves in front of Dexter. He'd given him an opportunity here, and he didn't want to fuck it up.

"Not exactly," Dexter said. "Just, you know, be cool. Jimmy is the guy you deliver to. Nobody else."

"Got it. Jimmy."

"All right, man. Don't stop for anything between here and there. Too much risk."

"Dude. I got to get gas."

"If you have to," Dexter said.

"You said this was simple."

"Simple is as simple does." Dexter's throat flexed as if he was about to say something else.

"Are you fucking Forrest Gump?" Crate said.

"I'm beginning to regret this."

"Now, don't. I can do this."

"You better be able to." Dexter thought for a moment.

"Shit. I'll make the run with you."

"No need," Crate said. "I got this." Crate had second thoughts, honestly. Third thoughts, even. But now he had to go through with it. The thoughts of bills paid, a new coop for the dog, new brakes and tires on both vehicles. A nice place he could take Jeanelle to.

"All right. Here goes." Dexter tossed him the package. "Stick it under your seat and go. Bring me back the money."

"I'm on it, Dex. And thanks."

"Don't thank me," Dexter said quickly.

*　*　*

Crate tucked the package under his seat. He figured it contained pills. He'd always known what Dex was into, so this came as no surprise, particularly the way things were these days. If it wasn't pills, it was meth, or something worse like heroin. Everybody had their crutch. Today people were more open about their pill addictions. Opioid epidemic my ass, Crate thought. What it is is a pain epidemic, and no way for most people to deal with it. He turned down the visor of his car and retrieved his sunglasses. It seemed hotter and brighter than ever.

He drove across the border into New York, trees surrounding him, an occasional gas truck rumbling by, but they were few and far between even now. The gas boom had come and gone, and people still clung to the idea of hitting it rich off their land even when the frackers had already gone in under the neighbors land and pulled it out anyway. No gas left, no industry left, pop. People like Dexter, who had been employed by Chesapeake, now had to sell pills to make money.

Crate took side streets whenever he could, trying to stay off the main road for fear of getting stopped. Most of the way involved I-81, so he couldn't really avoid cops. A trickle of sweat slid down his arm. Simple, he thought. Like delivering a pizza. He thought of Jeanelle. She'd like the money, but not the idea of him delivering pills. He'd have to keep the money safe somewhere and bleed it out over several weeks, so she wouldn't suspect something. He had to get on and help Cal or get a second job somewhere to justify the extra money. He'd end up having to work even harder to fake making money. Damn. He glanced at his phone. The GPS told him he had about twenty minutes before he came to the place where he was to meet Jimmy. Only Jimmy.

Crate pulled the Escort into a strip mall parking lot. The sun had about set, and shadows grew in the short pine trees growing in the mulched split between lots. He eased into a spot next to a 2018 Lexus in front of a tattoo parlor and a Granny's Pizza Palace. The address matched the pizza place. Unsure of what to do next, Crate sat there for a moment, then thrust his heel into the floorboards to put the package inside his pants, hanging his shirt over it. At the front window, he could see a man sitting, the only one in the pizza place. Fuck it.

He got up and went inside. The smell of dough and the sound of '80s music smacked him right in the face. Good smells, if not exactly comforting. "You know where I can find Jimmy?" he said.

The cashier looked him up and down. "Why? You looking for a job?"

"Yeah. He told me to show up. Tell him Dexter Moore sent me." Crate stuffed his hands inside his pockets. He'd expected something else. A house. An apartment building. Not a pizza place.

"Huh. Jimmy's next door. On his lunch break. Tell him we're getting busy over here." The man turned away, and Crate left.

The front door of the tattoo parlor hung heavy with a bead curtain on the inside that rattled when he opened it. Inside, the atmosphere was all metal and plastic, very uncomfortable, the kind of doctor-like atmosphere that gave Crate the nervous twitches. On a white table sat two thick books. One man waited, reading a magazine. Soon the tattoo artist came out. He stood easily a foot over Crate and maybe three hundred pounds, a tall, thick giant, covered in ink except for his face and neck. "What can I do for ya?" the man said. "I'm Mack, the artist."

"I'm looking for Jimmy," Crate said. Mack looked him over carefully, eyes narrowed. He jerked his head toward the back.

"Jimmy's back there, in the break room." Crate wondered why the manager of the pizza place got to take his break in the tattoo parlor, but figured he wasn't getting paid to think. He was getting paid to deliver. Crate entered the back room just as a man exited the bathroom, zipping up. He too, was covered in tattoos, and wore the same red shirt the cashier in the pizza place wore.

"Who the fuck are you?" the man said.

"Dexter Moore sent me," Crate said. "You got somewhere we can talk?"

"Open your mouth," Jimmy said. "Or I'll stomp your ass."

"Back up," Crate said. "I got a delivery for you." He motioned to Jimmy. "You sure you want to do it here?"

"I don't know you or motherfuck anything," Jimmy said. "Get your ass out the door." Mack came back through the door.

"Keep it down. I got clients out here." Mack barely paid attention to Crate, his eyes flicking over him briefly as he addressed Jimmy.

"Come on out back," Jimmy said. He pointed to a steel door next to the bathroom. Crate took a deep breath and followed Jimmy outside. They paused beside a small dumpster. Mack, behind Crate, suddenly clamped his arms behind him in a viselike grip.

"The fuck?" Crate managed to say, just before Jimmy hit him in the gut, nearly doubling him over. Then the blows came hard and heavy to his chest and gut and arms, again and again.

"Hold him up, Mack," Jimmy said, as if from far away. Crate hung limp in the huge man's arms. He'd puked, and his chest felt as if it had been stomped by elephants. "I'd hit you right in your motherfucking stupid face if I didn't have to make pizzas all night," Jimmy said. Mack let Crate go and he tumbled to his knees, retching. Crate reached into his pants and felt

Mack kick him in the stomach, and the package fell to the ground, where Jimmy picked it up. "You are a stupid motherfucker. Tell Dexter he needs to come himself next time, or we're going to have a bigger problem with him than we just demonstrated with you. Jam a two-by-four up his skinny ass and break it off."

Mack knelt down next to Crate, who gasped for breath, and put a hand on his back. "Stay down. You'll be fine in a few minutes. Then get out of here."

The entire thing took maybe ten minutes. Crate collapsed into a ball and passed out.

* * *

The strip mall lights kicked on at 9 p.m. and Crate woke up. It had been nearly an hour since he'd had the piss beaten out of him by Jimmy and Mack, and walking around the front, he could see the tattoo place was closed, but the pizza place did a roaring business. Six or seven cars parked in the lot, a whole crowd of people in the place. He couldn't start something even if he'd been capable. Twice in two days people had hit him. There would not be a third time. Crate took stock of himself. A rib twinged, and his chest felt like someone had hollowed him out from the inside. They'd left his face alone, but he'd be feeling the effects of this for days, if not weeks. And he had to come home to Jeanelle and Jefferson. And he'd have to explain to Dexter why he didn't have any money for the pills. He unlocked his Escort and felt under the seat. For some reason his jaw ached. All those body shots. What the hell would he say to Jeanelle? As if on cue, his phone vibrated, and he ignored it.

He took the drive back slowly, listening to the '80s station on the radio. He had no reason to worry about getting stopped at 9:30 at night, but he looked at every exit for a cop anyway, force of habit. He stopped in Elmira at a 7-Eleven for a six-pack of beer, texting Jeanelle at the same time, but didn't crack one until he sat in his driveway, car engine ticking. Outside the house, the door light kicked on, and he took half a beer down in one swallow and sighed. He closed the door behind him softly, as Jefferson lay sleeping in his swing. Jeanelle sat in the chair, arms crossed.

"So?" Jeanelle said softly. He steeled himself. She was such a good woman, and he'd fucked up.

"Dexter gave me some stuff to deliver up to Syracuse. Some guys. They took a disliking to me, and I couldn't tell them what they wanted to hear, so they tuned me up a little."

"Tuned you up." Jeanelle got up and crossed the carpet, touching his shoulders. "Are you hurt bad?"

"They pretty much stayed in the body," Crate said, wincing as her hands traced his ribs. She lifted his shirt.

"You're red," she said. "You're going to bruise up pretty bad. Are you going to work?"

"I don't have much choice, do I?"

"Does Dexter know?" Jeanelle's voice had taken an edge.

"Not yet. I should probably drive over there."

"You don't have what he needs." It wasn't a question, but he answered it anyway.

"No," Crate said. "I don't."

"How much money?" Jeanelle said.

"I don't know. They were supposed to give me an envelope to bring back."

"Oh, Crate." She took his hand. "Deal with it tomorrow."

"I better do it tonight," Crate said. "Bad news doesn't wait well." He drained the rest of his beer and tossed the can into the open garbage. He walked haltingly over to the refrigerator and deposited the rest of the beer. On the top shelf was a dinner plate covered in foil. "I'll eat that when I get home." He turned, wincing, back to the door. "I'm sorry, Jean," he said. He heard her sigh as he walked out into the night air. The bug zapper next door sounded.

*　*　*

Crate drove over the back roads to Dexter's house for the second time that night. The moon shone round and full in the sky, and all the lights were on in Dexter's house. By the time he'd reached the porch, the lights had gone off, except for the porch. Dexter stepped out to meet him.

"Hey," Crate said.

"I already heard," Dexter said. "That cocksucker Jimmy had me on the phone in minutes. They mess you up bad?"

"I don't know. I got a bad feeling about the ribs, but nothing I can't deal with."

"I got a bigger problem, now," Dexter said. "The fuck did you say?"

"I asked for Jimmy. They sent me to that tattoo parlor. The artist and this Jimmy dude fucked my shit up and took the package."

"Did he say why?" Dexter lit a cigarette, his fingers trembling. Crate could tell now he was out of his mind.

"I guess he didn't like the way I talk," Crate said.

Dexter snorted. "No. I guess not." He blew smoke out his nostrils. "This shit will not flush, Crate."

"I got to get home, Dex. I'll get you some money. To make up for it. It's just going to take some time."

"Nah, nah," Dexter said, flipping his hand. "We're going to have to settle this shit soon."

"How do you mean?"

"I mean we're going to go up there and reason with the motherfuckers." Dexter lifted his shirt and revealed the butt of a handgun.

"Oh no," Crate said. "I can't do shit like that anymore. I got a family."

"I got a girl too. I probably got kids, too, all over this county and the next. They have my money. If don't take it to them, I'm weak. I can't be weak." Dexter fondled the gun.

Crate shook his head. "No. Uh-uh. I have to work to-morrow."

"You can work the whole fucking week, I don't care. We go this weekend."

"Shit, Dex."

"Gird your loins, motherfucker. I told you we weren't playing." Dexter tossed the cigarette butt into a planter, joining a bunch of others. "Go home and get some sleep. I'll text you. On Friday."

"What am I going to tell Jeanelle?"

"Fucked if I know. Tell her the same thing I tell Caitlin. Nothing."

Dexter turned his back and closed the door. The last light in the house winked out, and Crate heard him stumbling around in the dark. Idiot. Off the porch, peepers sounded, and for a moment, Crate remembered being a kid and sleeping out in the yard, hearing the same thing and wondering at what point in the night they'd stop. He tried to stay up all night then to find out but fell asleep, and that was the way he felt right now. His stomach seized. His old life came up in his throat, and he choked it back.

* * *

He took the long way home, and by the time he'd made it back it was nearly 1:00 a.m. and he had to be at work at 4:00, so he said fuck it. Up all night. Jeanelle had turned off all the lights but the living room and the bare bulb over the door. He clanged the screen door shut and the new puppy nosed at his feet. He let him out briefly to shit before settling down with a single beer and a bottle of water. Turning the TV on, he found some MMA reruns from years past and picked the dog up into his lap. The dog hit his stomach with all four paws and Crate nearly heaved, he was in so much pain.

Crate knew tomorrow would be brutal, beat up and with no sleep, so he took the beer down quickly, then the water. The puppy stuck his nose up for a scratch. What would the weekend bring? He wouldn't feel any better by then, and Dexter would expect him to go in and try to kick these guys' asses or worse. It'd be big talk for Dexter, that skinny Shaggy-looking mother-fucker, but the real thing for Crate. And there was that big tattoo artist to think about. They couldn't break in there like criminals—don't disrespect the pizza joint—so it was hard to know what exactly Dexter had in mind. They'd have to have a plan, and Dexter didn't plan much, so that left Crate. Planning was not his strong suit, either.

It made sense to try to hit them at home, rather than the pizza place or the tattoo parlor, but then there'd be wives and kids and girlfriends to think of. The only thing to do, Crate decided, would be to hit them somewhere in between. He took another sip of the water and opened his eyes. On screen, the fighters clinched on the cage, the bigger man working inside with wild elbows, and the smaller man took one on the chin and crumpled in place. He closed his eyes again momentarily and felt Jean's weight settle on the cushion next to him.

"I know you don't want to hear this," Jeanelle said.

"Then just don't say it."

"We can figure something out. We can borrow money from Cal."

"Sure. 'Cal—need to borrow some money. For a drug deal I fucked up.' That won't work, Jean."

"He doesn't have to know what it's for."

"He's going to know." Crate's head thumped against the back of the couch. "I'm a fuckup."

"No, you're not," Jeanelle said. "You're a hardworking man who supports his family the right way."

"I used to be."

"This will pass. Don't let what you used to be fuck up the now. I need you. Jeff needs you. This stupid dog needs you." Jeanelle grabbed his arm. "Don't let Dexter fuck your life up. It's his money. Let him deal."

"He trusted me to do a job. I fucked it up. Now I need to make it right."

"We will. We'll get the money."

"It's not about the money. Dexter counted on me. I need to fix this."

"For Christ's sake, Creighton. Listen to yourself." Crate stayed silent and let her breath come heavy. She sighed. "I'm going to bed."

Crate took the dog by the scruff and deposited him on the floor. The interviewer on the TV shoved a mic into a bloody fighter's face, who spoke and gestured to the camera with one finger, shaking it. Crate set the alarm on his phone for 4:30 a.m. He could get two hours of sleep and push it, still get to work on time.

* * *

By two in the afternoon, Crate had caught his second wind. He'd been able to skate by the first part of the day breaking rocks and now it was down to learning to operate a loader, which took up time and didn't put much strain on his stomach muscles. He had lots of time to think about how Dexter might handle the situation this weekend. He'd go in balls to the wall, Crate figured, and get them both hurt or killed. He'd have to let Dexter take the lead, but he couldn't let it get out of hand, either. No good, either way. He angled the bucket into a pile of #4 gravel and rammed it in, rocks spilling off the side. He dumped the partial and reloaded, as he'd been heavy on the right-hand side and got a more balanced load, which he turned and deposited in a waiting dump truck. He had five minutes before another truck showed up, so he set the brake and got out of the loader to piss.

He wondered if Dexter had any notion of bringing someone else in to support them. Dexter, skinny and pale, wasn't exactly intimidating except in his crazy eyes and they'd already beat the shit out of Crate, so it only made sense, but then someone else would know Dexter's business. He'd just have to wait and see how Dexter played it. The rest of the afternoon passed without incident, and he greased the loader, washed up, and left. On the way home, he stopped at a grocery store and bought a bouquet of some flowers for Jeanelle and a stuffed puppy for Jeff. He didn't have to be a fuckup.

When Crate arrived at the trailer, he saw Cal's truck parked next to Jeanelle's. He swore under his breath, reefed himself out of the cab angrily, and felt a rib pop. He put a hand on his side before he'd thought about it. Jeanelle had tied the dog to the cinder block steps with a length of chain, and he'd already run a half-circle of grass down to the dirt. He paused with the flowers, and scratched the dog's head, then went inside.

"Hi, baby," Jeanelle said, holding out her hands. "They're beautiful. Thank you." Cal sat in the recliner, hands clasped, a sweating can of beer on the table. Crate bent down and gave the stuffed puppy to Jeff, who smelled its head briefly then abandoned it to play with a set of plastic rings.

"So what brings you here, Cal?" Crate said, opening the fridge for his own beer.

"All right. I'll come to the point. Jeanelle says you need money. I'm not going to ask why. She says you need it, and her mother and I are in a position to help. Once. I gave Jeanelle a thousand dollars. Consider it an interest-free loan to be repaid when you can."

"Give him back the money, Jeanelle." Crate cracked open the beer.

"Can I talk to you alone?" Jeanelle said.

"I don't want to get into this," Cal said, standing up. "I'm going to go see your mother."

"Thank you, Cal," Jeanelle said.

"Give him back the fucking money, Jean." Crate sat down.

"Once," Cal said, and slammed the door behind him.

"Now I owe two people," Crate said. "Fucking great."

"But you can pay off Dexter now."

"That doesn't make me any less a punk," Crate said. "I still have to go see those guys. And now I owe Cal a grand. I'm twice fucked."

"But better to owe Cal than Dexter. You don't have to do anything else illegal."

"Yeah I do."

"Can't you try to give Dexter the money?"

"The money's not the issue. Now Dexter looks weak. Now I look weak. Dexter especially can't afford that, and I'm the one who made him look that way. There's no way this gets better." Crate opened another beer and drained it, then opened another. "Now please leave me be for a minute." Jeanelle looked at him sharply and gathered Jeff and the diaper bag up in one hand and left.

"Where you going?" Crate yelled after her, but heard nothing but the truck door slam.

* * *

By the time Jeanelle returned Crate had calmed down and stopped drinking; he wanted a clear head for the argument he knew was coming. Jeanelle had turned the truck off and sat in the seat with her head leaned back for a long moment as Crate watched her from the living room window where he'd been anxiously awaiting her.

She banged through the front door and without a word handed him the baby, who gurgled and slapped at Crate, happy to see him. Crate was happy too, as the baby gave him something to concentrate on other than the mess he was in with Dexter and now with Jeanelle. Crate took a sniff and knew the baby needed changing, so he laid him down on the couch and took care of business. By the time he'd finished Jeanelle had come out from the bedroom, the color in her cheeks high. Crate set the baby on the ground, where he immediately toddled over to the dog and started pulling at his ears, which the dog took in good humor.

"So I did it," Jeanelle said, sitting down near Jeff, her hand trailing his hair.

"Did what now?" Crate said, careful with his tone.

"I took the money to Dexter." Jeanelle lit a cigarette from a new pack. He hadn't known her to smoke in the five years they'd been married. She might as well have announced she was from another planet. The news was that bad.

"Why did you do that?" Crate said.

"Because I didn't think you would do it," Jeanelle said.

"I can't do it," Crate yelled. "You might just as well have handed him my balls."

"I did it for Jeff. For us. You don't have to do anything now."

"Jesus," Crate said. "You fucked this up good." As if on cue, Crate's phone buzzed. "You know this is Dexter," Crate said. "This ain't ever going to be done now." He looked at the phone. "COME OVER," the text read. No hey man. No nothing. Just about what he'd expected.

"He's got his money," Jeanelle said. "Now he needs to leave you alone." On the floor, the puppy yelped and snapped at the baby, and Jeanelle picked Jeff up as he began to howl, more out of surprise than hurt.

"You think this is simple, Jean." He shook the phone at her. "I'm into him now worse than I was."

"No you're not." Jeanelle swayed the baby back and forth on her hip, Jeff sobbing now in hiccups.

"Yes. I am." Crate stuffed the phone into his pocket and picked up his keys, stopping first in the bedroom for his .357, which he shoved into the front of his pants and hung a flannel shirt over so Jean wouldn't see. "I'm going up there to fix this now," Crate said, slamming the door behind him. Outside, the sun had drawn down into a simmering orange ball, and he headed in its opposite direction. Toward Dexter.

*　*　*

On the way over, he rehearsed what he would say to Dexter. They needed to hit them tonight. Crate needed to be done with this. They could drive up to the pizza place and reason this out man-to-man. If it went sour, Crate could scare them with the .357, but he had no intention of shooting anyone or even bringing it out. Having it gave him, not confidence exactly—he knew better than that, from the bad old days—but the knowledge that if he played everything right, he could be out from under this huge thing he'd gotten himself into.

He turned into Dexter's driveway and swore under his breath.: Robbie Moore's truck was parked next to Dexter's crotch rocket. A bad sign. Crate hoped it was his girlfriend come to visit Dexter's woman, but he knew it wouldn't be. His luck couldn't be that good. Sure enough, as he turned off the ignition, Dexter and Robbie stepped out onto the porch, Robbie in the same stupid cowboy hat he'd worn when fighting Crate over the pup.

"Hello, Crate," Dexter said, a turn in his voice. "Jeanelle already paid me off. Kinda surprised to see you here."

"Anybody'd send a woman to do his work for him. . .," Robbie began.

"Shut up," Dexter said. "Now what do you want?"

"First off, I didn't send Jeanelle. She got the money and came by herself. I didn't know a thing about it," Crate said. Robbie snorted and Crate turned toward him. "Look. I got something I need to talk with Dexter about. Can you take a hike?" Robbie and Dexter exchanged glances.

"You can talk in front of Robbie. He's my main man," Dexter said. Crate ignored that crack. He'd been under the impression he was Dexter's main man, but then, it seemed as if he might have been played again.

"Fine," Crate said. "I want to hit those guys tonight."

"Jeanelle paid me off," Dexter said. "She led me to understand you were done with me."

"Well, I'm not." His ribs twinged. "Those guys beat the piss out of me. They took the package."

"Jesus Christ, Crate. It wasn't a package. It was pills. Pills I can't sell now, and money I didn't have until your wife gave it to me, no thanks to you, and now I have to deal with people thinking my word is shit. Trust. You can't buy it right now." Dexter spit into the planter.

"That's why I'm here. I'm done talking. Let's go up there tonight when that pizza place closes and hit them."

"And do what exactly?"

"Get my money," Crate said. "They'll have enough deposited to make up for the money Jean gave you. We split the money fifty-fifty. It looked like a busy place, and I know from their website they're cash only and open till 1 a.m. If we hit them about 1:45 we should be fine."

"You want to rob them?"

"Didn't they rob you? Us? Probably broke a rib on me. It's not robbery. They owe me, and we're going to collect." Crate folded his arms.

"You believe this guy?" Dexter said. "This sounds like the old Crate, back when he was a bad old boy."

"I don't trust a man gets his ass kicked twice in a week," Robbie said.

"You didn't kick my ass," Crate said. "I quit. There's a difference."

"How do we know you're not going to quit halfway tonight?" Robbie said.

"So it's we now?" Crate asked. Dexter's silence answered him.

"Three-way split," Robbie said.

"Done," Crate said.

"So what do we do until 10 or so?" Robbie said.

"I can think of some things to do," Dexter said. "I got a fistful of Adderall and enough 5.56 to choke a horse. Let's shoot some barrels till dark."

"All right," Robbie said. "I got some roll-up earplugs in my glove box." Crate simply nodded. The whole night returned him to the man he'd been ten years ago, before Jeanelle, before Jeff, before he'd had a real job and something to lose. It felt bad, honestly, but he knew if they pulled it off, he'd have the money back to repay Cal and then some. Jeanelle's voice came to him then, but he pushed it back in his mind.

* * *

"Pow! I gutted that fucker," Robbie said, bringing the AR-15 down from his shoulder. Sure enough, about thirty yards out, the 55-gallon drum Dexter had filled sloshed water from fifteen holes before Dexter grabbed the rifle from him.

"Watch this," Dexter said, pulling the rifle smoothly up. *Bap-bap-bap-bap.* The reports echoed down the ridge, and Crate dug the plugs from his ears. In the sudden silence somewhere downhill a dog howled, and the sun was nearly gone.

"We about killed it," Robbie said, tipping his cowboy hat back. "Crate, are you going to take a knock at it?"

"Nah, I'm good." Crate could feel the weight of the .357 dragging the front of his drawers down.

"Suit yourself," Dexter said, his eyes glittering. "Let's go inside and hook up the PlayStation. That *Fallout 4* kicks some ass."

"Dogmeat," Robbie said.

"Fucking aye," Dexter said. "That fucker sticks by you. I've never had a dog like him." He thrust the disc into the station.

"That's because most dogs don't care as long as you feed them," Robbie said, jostling the controller up and down in his hand.

"Not right," Crate said. "Dogs love just like people."

"Dogs love like people, he says." Dexter said. "You're the strangest fucker, Crate."

Just then Dexter's girlfriend Caitlin stepped into the room. She came over and sat on Dexter's lap and looked deep into his eyes. "Hooboy. You're wired for sound."

"Damned straight," Dexter said, grabbing her around the waist and pulling her close. "I need a come-down."

"Not with these boys here," Caitlin said. Crate thought of Jeanelle.

"We're going to see a man about a horse," Dexter said, getting up and pulling Caitlin by the hand. "You guys keep yourselves loose." Crate closed his eyes briefly and opened them again to watch Caitlin's ass as she walked into the other room with Dexter and immediately felt guilty.

"I'll be damned," Robbie said, his eyes distant. "He's got two characters in here, one named Dexter and one named Fuckhead."

"Play under Fuckhead," Crate suggested. Robbie snorted and started the game.

* * *

About 1:00 a.m they'd parked in the adjoining strip mall to Granny's Pizza and the tattoo parlor. Robbie had gone into the tattoo parlor under pretense of getting a tattoo and reported that the big fucker, Mack, who'd helped beat up Crate, was not in fact working. Instead, he'd found a slim woman with jet-black hair and piercings all up and down her face doing the art. This was a good sign, Crate thought. They pulled masks over their faces and Robbie left his goddamned cowboy hat in the car.

Crate went first, heart in his throat, Dexter and Robbie close behind. They staked out the back door and hit it when Jimmy came out to empty the fryer grease.

"You don't know what you're doing," Jimmy said. Crate pulled the .357 from his front and heard Dexter mutter under his breath.

"Give us the money, motherfucker," Robbie said, pushing Jimmy in the chest. Crate motioned to Jimmy with the gun, trying his best not to speak and reveal his voice. Jimmy went in and popped the register with a press to the No Sale button. Crate stuffed the money into a backpack without counting it. "Now the safe," he said in a low, rough voice.

"Motherfucker, this ain't all pizza money. You are going to have some serious problems if you fuck me over."

"Just open the safe," Robbie said. Crate poked the man in the head with the .357, cocked it. Jimmy quailed, and on his knees, prodded open the safe with shaky fingers. Crate took all the bills with one hand still holding the gun on Jimmy, large bills first, most of them fixed with rubber bands, but some with the paper bank bands still on them. Dexter flipped his hand in a "come on" motion. Crate handed Robbie the gun then took a roll of duct tape out of the pack and expertly hauled Jimmy's arms behind his back and fixed them with the tape, stuffing an old rag in his mouth and taping it shut. He layered his legs the same way while Dexter and Robbie stood there trembling. He uncocked the weapon and stuffed it back in his pants. They left and slammed the back door shut. All told it had taken maybe fifteen minutes. Jimmy'd get out of the tape, but it would be a while, and by that time they'd be on their way back home, sailing down I-81 with a load of cash.

"God *damn*, Crate. I didn't know you had it in you. That went slick as piss." Dexter held the bag in his hand, counting. They'd tossed the masks in a nearby dumpster and Robbie had put the goddamned cowboy hat on again. He sat in the back seat jiggling his leg against Crate's seat.

"Would you quit your diddling?" Crate said. "You're killing my back."

"How much?" Robbie said, rubbing his hands together.

"Looks like a little more than $4,400," Dexter said. "Hot damn. We're gonna pull this off."

"I swear, Crate. If I'd known—" Robbie began.

"For Christ's sake, Robbie. Shut up." Crate kept his hands on the wheel. "Divide that shit up. Even number of bills each. Rounds out to just under $1,500 each. I'm keeping the loose change." Neither of the men argued with him.

"The best part is, they don't even know it was us," Robbie said.

"I wouldn't count on it," Crate said. "I just want you to know. Both of you. If you ever breathe a word about this I'm coming for you. Because I'm never doing this again." Neither man spoke aloud, but Crate caught them exchanging glances. He'd have to deal with them later. He'd dealt with worse inside, though. And suddenly, like a bucket of water dropped on him from above, he was in it. All over again, with so much more to lose. He'd be looking over his shoulder for the rest of his life now. Again.

TELL THE MAN ABOUT LOVE

Jim Messner took a step to the side as Dickey Jones slashed the knife just past his nose, jamming his fist into Dickey's throat but it didn't do much damage. The light faded under the trees, and music spilled out from the open windows of Putnam Park.

"Goddamn the goddamned thing," Dickey said as he took another drunken swipe. "Stand still, ya little bastard."

Good thing Dickey was drunk. The knife looked shiny and sharp, and as much as he enjoyed fucking Dickey's wife, Suzanne, Jim wasn't willing to die for her, which said as much about their relationship as anything Suzanne had ever said to him in the heat of sex. "Dickey," Jim said. "I wish you'd be reasonable about this."

Dickey swiped a hand across his beard. "I don't want a divorce."

"But Suzanne might."

"I swear I don't know what she sees in you. It sure ain't your giant dick or your brass balls." Dickey crouched again. "Now stand still." Jim took a step back as Dickey thrust the knife at him again, a lock-blade Buck better used for gutting deer. He grabbed Dickey's wrist and twisted it upward and around. Dickey went to his knee, and Jim kicked him hard in the belly, which spilled Dickey onto his side clutching his middle and left Jim holding the knife. He locked the blade back into the haft and threw it up onto the shingled roof of Putnam Park. Some enterprising soul would retrieve it for Dickey later, Jim was sure, but for the time being he was safe.

Normally a knife fight would have attracted the entire bar and the state police besides, but Dickey hadn't let Jim even get to the door, so people had just started to notice. He knelt beside Dickey, who had a line of spittle dripping into his beard, and left a hand on his shoulder. "Do yourself a favor, Dickey. Don't get up, and don't come after me." He fished around in Dickey's jeans pocket and threw his keys up onto the roof with the knife. Then Jim ripped off Dickey's shoes and tossed them up there too. It would be several minutes before Dickey would be able to gather himself, and that gave Jim time to get the hell out.

Jim turned his truck right out of the Park and drove toward Suzanne and Dickey's house. Not the smartest move, maybe, but he felt as if he owed it to Suzanne to tell her. He drove with his knee and tapped a quick message into his mobile phone. *Kicked Dickey's ass. Coming 2 C U.*

* * *

Jim drove up the long hill, roadside gathered in shadow with larch and poplar lining the ditch, and wheeled into Suzanne and Dickey's driveway. He shut the truck off to the sound of Poochie and Cooter, Dickey's two redbones, baying at him from their doghouses cemented to the side of the pole barn. The front porch light was on, which was Suzanne's usual signal that it was safe to come by. The house opened up into the kitchen, the walls covered in hammered-flat tin cans and old license plates, some of which were for decoration and others for insulation from Dickey's frequent rages which had left holes. The kitchen, though, was Suzanne's, and the rest of the house, rough, poor, but spotlessly clean.

"I'm in here, Jim," Suzanne called from the living room. She sat in near darkness, the only light coming from the lamp on the end table. Jim sat next to her and put his hand on her knee. "How bad?" she said.

"I'm all right," Jim said. "I took his knife and shoes away from him to buy some time."

"I mean how bad is he hurt?" Suzanne said, brushing a hand through her blonde hair.

"I kicked him in the belly. He's going to be sore. You need to pack a bag."

"Already done." Suzanne gestured to the other side of the table, where she'd laid a small suitcase and another shoulder bag.

"That ain't going to be enough," Jim said.

"I'm coming back for the rest of my stuff tomorrow."

"He's not going to be any less drunk tomorrow if you leave tonight. Probably drunker. You need to pack for a couple weeks."

"He'll be better in the morning."

"I kicked him in the gut and left him in the parking lot. He's not going to be using his good graces."

"He's never hit me before."

"Not yet. He hits the walls, the dogs, the truck dashboard. It ain't going to be long before he gets to you, especially now that he knows about us."

"Where do you expect me to go?"

Jim sighed. "I guess you can stay with me a few days."

"That's the best idea you have?" Suzanne chewed her pinky nail. "I need somewhere permanent."

"That's a hell of a thing to say to me."

"Jim. I've always known you and me weren't a forever thing," Suzanne said. "But I love you."

"Yes, but I can spot you a couple days until you find a shelter or something. What about your sister?"

"She can't stop Dickey. And you've proven you can. And you know Dickey keeps all that Oxy in the house. I can't have them here. Short of the cops, I guess you're my worst best bet."

"We should get moving," Jim said. Just then he heard the sound of a truck engine gunning up the hill's dirt road, gravel spattering as it ran. They had maybe five minutes to get out.

"I guess you shocked him sober," Suzanne said.

"Let's go," Jim said, grabbing her suitcase and bag. Together they left, front door ajar. As Jim jumped into the driver's seat, he saw the plume of dust Dickey's truck had developed like a tail behind him down the road a piece. Suzanne slammed the door beside him.

"Go go go," she yelled, and Jim tore out of the driveway to the sound of the dogs barking and banged the truck into second gear before he'd gotten fifty yards down the hill. He figured he could get maybe a half-mile head start before drunk Dickey realized it was him and Suzanne. Either way, he headed straight down the road, Suzanne holding onto the side of the bucket seat and the door. He hit fifty miles an hour and roared past Dickey. In the rearview, Jim saw Dickey whip around to follow them.

Jim knew Dickey wouldn't want to get popped for a DWI, so he deliberately went past the places on 660 where he knew the state police sometimes sat looking for drunks. Sure enough, Dickey slowed down and Jim sped up, losing him on the track of back roads between Covington, Blossburg, and Arnot, driving the countryside guided only by moonlight and his own sense of impending trouble.

* * *

Suzanne's head lolled against the headrest and Jim eventually pulled into the Hampton Inn on the side of Route 15 in Mansfield. He woke Suzanne with a gentle shake and the two of them checked into a first-floor room. Jim cranked the AC while Suzanne showered, peering constantly out the thickly curtained window for Dickey's truck, even though there was no reasonable way he could know where they were and even if he did he'd be unlikely to kick up a storm in a public place. Sober, that is.

Jim stretched out on the bed and waited for Suzanne to finish. He closed his eyes for a moment and thought of the knife, then jumped up with Suzanne's bag in his hand. He went out to his truck and retrieved his .40 from under the seat, thrust it into the bag, and took it back into the hotel room. If Dickey would hit him, try to knife him, then the next logical step would be a gun. Be prepared, like the Boy Scouts said. He took the pistol and put it under the pillows on his side of the bed.

Suzanne came out, toweling her hair. She put on a nightgown and a pair of sweatpants, then lay down beside him, her breast heavy against his arm.

"How long you think before he shows up?" Suzanne said. She tipped a bottle of wine into her throat.

"I hope he's sleeping it off somewhere," Jim said.

"Huh. Not a fucking chance," Suzanne said, and closed her eyes. "I give it an hour."

* * *

The early morning found Jim semi-comfortable, Suzanne's head resting on his half-asleep arm, both of them nude now. He'd hoped the whir of the air conditioner would lull him to sleep, but the thought of Dickey coming after him prevented it. He shifted slightly and felt the hardness of the .40 under his head. If Dickey came, he'd know what to do. Try to scare the dumb fucker off. Try to make him see that love wasn't worth dying for. The problem was, he didn't know if Dickey believed in love. The situation left Jim fucked, and with Suzanne's head still resting on him, he felt suddenly unsure of what to do. Outside, he saw the turn of headlights into the parking spot next to the truck with a screech of brakes. He shook Suzanne awake.

"Baby. He's out there." Jim swung out of bed retrieved his pistol from beneath the pillow and laid it on the bed. He pushed his feet into his pants, then his boots, and took the pistol up, checking the load. He hesitated for a moment, then held the gun tightly in his hand as he went out to meet Dickey. Suzanne would be safe in the room.

"Kill him," Suzanne said. "I'm tired of this shit."

"Jesus," Jim said. "You're awful drunk and you ain't pulling the trigger. I am."

"I've put up with his drug-dealing ass for ten years now. No more."

"I am not going to kill him for you," Jim said.

"Then why'd you bring the gun?"

"In case he tries to kill me first," Jim said. "Now can you please be quiet? Maybe I can convince him you're not here."

"Good luck with that," Suzanne said. Jim stuck the pistol in the front of his pants and walked out into the hallway. Just past the ice maker and the vending machine Jim found the door. He knew as soon as he stepped outside everything that happened would be on Dickey's terms. As long as he stayed inside, his life was his own. Outside, his life teetered between Dickey and Suzanne, and it was a fight he knew he'd lose, no matter which way it turned out. Yet as soon as he'd put the gun under his pillow, he'd made the decision. It was only left for him to follow through on it. He opened the door and walked out into the early morning air.

* * *

The sun shined just a bit over the hills, bathing them in dim light except for the spots where the halogen lot lights illuminated pockets of asphalt in a hard glare. Leaning on the truck, Dickey tipped a bottle into his mouth.

"Still drinking, Dickey?" Jim moved to Dickey's right, into the landscaped shrubbery, away from his gun hand.

"Wouldn't do any good to stop now," Dickey said. "I take it she's in there."

"Nope. I dropped her off at her sister's."

"You're a piss-poor liar."

"She doesn't want to see you."

"I know that." Dickey tipped the bottle up again, then set it on the hood of the truck. "I don't want her seeing you."

"You don't have any control over what she does now," Jim said.

"Does she want a divorce?"

"Dickey, I don't have clue one what the woman wants."

"She wants you."

"For now."

"Do you love her?" Dickey crossed his arms.

Jim considered carefully what he was about to say. "I'm very fond of her."

"Oh for fuck's sake. That's a no, then."

"No. It's the truth."

"Goddamn it. I didn't even lose out to true love. I lost out to fondness."

"You lost out because you drink yourself stupid every night."

"What's your excuse then?"

Jim laughed. "I don't have one."

"All right, enough of this shit," Dickey said, standing up straight and nearly stumbling. He took a pistol from his belt as Jim drew and brought the gun to bear on Dickey's chest, but Dickey didn't raise his. Instead he let it slip loose from his fingers onto the pavement. Jim lowered his hand.

"What do you want?" Jim said. Dickey turned his hands up, imploring.

"Just shoot me," Dickey said. "I can't take this shit anymore." The side door of the hotel slammed open and Suzanne came out, dressed in her night clothes, but carrying her little pack of clothes and suitcase. Dickey howled and went to his knees to pick up the gun. He brought it up and squeezed a shot off at Jim, who took careful aim and shot Dickey in the chest, the smack of the bullet into flesh followed by the loud report deafening him. Jim watched Dickey fall sideways, his head thumping onto the pavement, before he realized he was bleeding himself. He went numb.

Suzanne went white, clasping her arms to herself. "Oh, honey," she said.

Jim didn't know which of them she referred to, but later on in the back of the police cruiser, he had time to reflect. His gun arm now heavily bandaged and throbbing, he thought it probably didn't matter much. Dickey wanted to be shot. Jim had killed a man. Nothing could ever change that.

Suzanne stood outside with a blanket around her shoulders, the flashing lights giving her a spectral glow, talking with a state police officer. When the door finally opened and the officer spoke to Jim, he found himself wanting to tell him about love, about what it was and wasn't, but he opened his mouth and nothing came out.

THE KEEPER

I had to deliver the weed to Fuzzy Zemanek at the midway point of the Tioga County Fair. Fuzzy had committed himself to the public good at the petting zoo all day, scraping up shit and making sure the hand dispensers were full of antibacterial soap. They had a lion cub and a bunch of rabbits, a llama, three goats, and a bunch of these dirty-looking zebras. I hated zebras. Fuzzy sold his weed in the back, alongside the pocket snappers, black snakes, and firecrackers, nothing bigger than a quarter stick. I had a lunch sack full of baggies stuffed with weed. It doesn't seem like much but Fuzzy's supplier, John, who was also my boss, had a lot of little businesses that added up to a lot.

Fuzzy had a password for weed sales. You had to say "Where's the good stuff?" Then he'd take you behind the petting zoo into the zebra trailer, where he had all the contraband stored neatly in plastic bags of various sizes in cardboard boxes, and you know, do his thing.

I'd brought him weed before many times, but usually at his house in Wellsboro, and this new arrangement made me antsy. I didn't like horses, cows, llamas, or especially zebras. Everything on hooves made me nervous, and the human crowd would be huge today, relatively speaking, all of them blissed out on the gospel stylings of Cletus Barnhill, who was playing concerts this afternoon and tonight. No place to make a dope deal, but my boss said we'd make out like we were selling salvation if Fuzzy could work his end.

I drove up from Mansfield to the fairgrounds in Joseph's new blue F-150. He'd been making money hand over fist since giving up the farmer act and becoming the outlaw he'd always thought he was, playing Hank Williams III loud and getting a concealed carry permit. He didn't grow the stuff that I knew of, but he always had bags of it siphoned out of somebody's stash and stored in outdoor caches in four different counties in two different states. He liked being the smart one in town, always well-to-do and showing it. I liked being his hired man. But those zebras. Dirty, ugly, diseased, warp-faced, wall-eyed motherfuckers. Why people let their children near them was anybody's guess.

The parking lot was chock-full of cars. The only place I could park was on the road across the way from the fairgrounds, which made me nervous because I couldn't see the truck and if it came back with a scratch Joseph would try his best to cut my head off with words. Besides the sack of dope, there was also the troubling notions that Fuzzy had taken to regarding my girl, Karen. And, sad truth to tell, I think she liked the potential drama. So I might bust somebody's nose today.

The chicken pens were all closed due to nameless overseas diseases sweeping farms in the state, but I could tell by the smell the 4-H hog lots were in full swing, along with the rabbits that weren't part of the petting zoo. I recognized a good number of folks, most of whom seemed to be there for the concert, dressed up in their best clothes and colognes, women showing a lot of breast and leg. I thought maybe Joseph had miscalculated the demand for once. I wouldn't know until I talked to Fuzzy, who was selling a handful of goat kibble to a senior citizen.

"I've been waiting for like two hours," Fuzzy said, grabbing the bag from me.

"I got here as quick as I could," I said.

"Shut up, Jim. Not where everybody can hear." He motioned behind us, to the trailer, so I followed him back. Two boxes were filled with fireworks and a shoebox held some pot. "This isn't going to be enough," Fuzzy said. "Go get some more."

I hadn't looked in the bag, but I looked at what he had. "There's no way you're going to sell that."

"You wait. The stoners haven't even shown up yet."

"This is a tiny fair," I said. "You're not going to sell to these middle-aged fat fucks."

"That's hell of a thing to call your family," Fuzzy said, and pointed. Sure enough, my mom and dad and my girlfriend Karen had come in through the livestock pens. "Get lost," Fuzzy said. "And tell John I could have done a lot better by him if I'd got what I asked for." He handed me a wad of bills which I didn't bother to count. It wasn't my money, after all.

I left by going through the reptile exhibit. Some park ranger had an albino boa constrictor on display. I swear it hissed at me as I excused myself and passed the rest of the snakes, rattlers and copperheads and another boa constrictor all together in a steel tub. This way I could sneak up behind Karen and grab her ass. I had gotten within a few feet of her when some little shit threw a snapper at her bare and tanned legs. "Goddamn these brats," Karen said, swiping at a spot on her knee.

"Now, they don't mean anything, you know," Mom said.

"It still hurts," Karen said. Then she noticed me. "Oh, Jimmy!"

"You want me to hunt him down and spank him, baby? I'll do it, too," I said.

"I thought you were working today, Jim," Dad said. He lipped a cigarette out of his pack. "Or did you take the day off to come play?" Sarcasm was not my father's strong suit.

"I delivered some stuff people ordered," I said. "I'm heading back right now and getting my truck."

"Oh, let me come with you," Karen said. "If that's OK with you, Mrs. Riggs."

My mom looked pleased at being called Mrs. Riggs. "I think that's fine," Mom said.

"John Norman ain't getting any more work out of you today," Dad snorted. I ignored him and took Karen by the hand, hoping to get out without Dad saying anything else to cut my balls off in front of my girl. Just then I heard some raised voices at the petting zoo, then three shots one right after the other, people screaming their heads off and running around. I ran over to Fuzzy, dragging Karen by the hand.

Two ladies were flitting around Fuzzy, who lay on the ground holding his chest. I could hear from the wheezing that one of the shots had gotten a lung, a sucking wound spreading blood all over his white T-shirt. I glanced at the zebra trailer, and the bag of pot was gone. "Fuzzy, who was it?" Fuzzy looked up at me, eyes wide, frothy blood at his mouth, and the air just leaked out of him. His eyes remained open, lifeless, just like someone had turned out the light.

"Oh. My. God." Karen said, covering her mouth with her hand. One of the two ladies who'd bent over him passed out and thumped face-first onto the dirt. The other one pointed to the parking lot.

"He had a black watch cap on and a Hank Williams shirt," she said. "Should I dial nine eleven?"

"Yes, Ma'am, I would." I got up and ran toward the road hoping to see whatever vehicles were leaving the fairgrounds. Karen held her arms over her breasts and ran with me. I slipped a bit in my work boots, but I saw a red Chevy leave the lot and head toward Mansfield. I pointed Karen to John's truck, and we both got in, breathless. I started the engine and pulled out. In a minute or so we were doing seventy on the two-lane road trying to catch up, and I fumbled in the ashtray where I'd left my cell phone. It took me another minute to get John on the line.

"What's going on, Jim?" John said. "Did you deliver?"

"Fuzzy's dead, man. Somebody shot him."

"What?" John said. "Why'd they—oh fuck it. Did you deliver?"

"I did deliver, but five minutes later he was dead, man."

"That was the worst thing I've ever seen," Karen said. "The worst."

"Who is that with you?" John said.

"It's Karen."

"You're an idiot, Jim," he said. "Why did you—never mind. Do you know who shot him?"

"Some guy in a red Chevy with jacked-up wheels. Lady there said he was wearing a Hank Williams shirt and a black watch cap. I'm going to catch up with him soon. I'm doing eighty down the goddamn road."

"Slow down and come to the farm," John said. "Don't get pulled over."

"I got nothing on me. I delivered. If they pull me over all I'll get is a ticket."

"Just do what I say," John said. "There's a pistol under your seat."

"Jesus, John. Why didn't you tell me?"

"I didn't think you'd have to use it."

"Use it! I don't want to use it."

"You may have to yet," John said. "Get off the phone and come straight here." I thumbed the phone off and reached under the seat. Sure enough, I felt a towel with something heavy in it. I drove with my knee as I unwrapped a blued .357 Magnum.

"What are you doing with that?" Karen asked. "You're not going to shoot anybody."

"I'm trying to think." I'd never assumed in the midst of all the things I had to do as John Norman's hired man that I'd be packing a gun. I half-wrapped it again and put it back under the seat.

"Now your prints are on it." Karen shook her head. "This is all too much. Take me home."

"I'd have to shoot somebody first. And I'll wipe it off before we get to the farm." Then it came to me. "Karen—I know who did it!"

"Who was it?"

"It was a Proustman, I'm 95 percent sure they entered a truck like that into the pulling contest over in Chemung." The Proustmans were gentleman farmers from New Jersey, with a dairy farm the next county over that did poorly, but got them government grants anyway. There were three of them who lived there off and on, Jerry, Jeff, and the youngest and cockiest, Walker, who was a couple years older than me at twenty-three. I had my money on Walker.

"So what now?" Karen said, wiping her eyes. "Is he going to ask you to kill Walker?"

"No, I think he's going to ask me to get the pot back though," I said.

"Oh no. How is Mama Zemanek ever going to recover? She just lost her husband last year. Now Fuzzy, too?" Karen said. "Poor woman."

"I'm more afraid of what John's going to ask me to do."

"Just because he asks doesn't mean you have to do what he says." Karen's blue eyes snapped. "You can be a man without his approval."

"I have to have a job," I said. "John Norman pays really fucking well."

"What would your dad say?" Karen said.

"He's probably OK with it if it proves my manhood or some ridiculous shit."

"That's so stupid," Karen said. She put her hand on my arm. "You don't have to prove anything, especially to him. Or me. I'll protect you."

"Easier said than done, sweets." The road curved around the Updike place, a barn and a small house set in the swell of the valley between Stark Mountain and Tower Hill. The Norman farm was just up the hill, a small operation with about fifty cows and maybe 150 acres of mostly forest. I knew the territory as well as I knew my name. I'd been in every hollow and climbed every hill throughout boyhood and my young adulthood. John stood by my old truck as I turned in by the milkhouse.

"Jimmy, this is what needs to happen," John said. His words came in a rush from high in his chest. He felt the tension from the possibility of the shooting being connected with him. People thought highly of him in the county. I interrupted him with my ideas about the Proustmans. John rubbed his chin as he listened to me.

"Well," I said. "What do you think?"

"You can use your head for something more than a hat rack," John said. Karen grabbed my arm with both hands and squeezed. That was more praise than I'd ever heard from my old man in twenty-one years of being his son. "I think you're right. Now this is my plan." He began talking, and I listened. I was good at listening.

The way John broke it down, it would go like this: I would go in my truck with Karen and the .357, John would follow in his, and we would try to catch whichever one of those Proustman boys happened to be doing the nightly milking. We would brace him with the gun and force him to tell us which of the boys had ripped off the drugs and killed Fuzzy.

John, much to my disbelief, was more worried about the money he'd lost when Fuzzy didn't make the sales. He blamed that on the Proustmans, and after he got back his money or the drugs he said we could call the cops, forgetting I guess that I had already told the woman at the petting zoo to dial 911. Cops were on the way, I figured, and if we were going to get the money, we'd have to punch it to get to the Proustman farm in time. It was now 3:45. It would take us forty-five minutes to get to the crossroads at the top of Coryland Road in Bradford County, and we'd have to start now.

"I don't want necessarily to be party to this," Karen said, tying her hair back in a short ponytail, as if she was going to work some hard job. "Take me home."

"You're already party to this," I said as I started the truck, the .357 between Karen and me. Clearly she had already succumbed to fear; she shied away from the gun like it was an electric fence. "And you heard the plan, so you're an accessory to anything we do tonight."

Karen crossed her arms and looked out the window. I put a hand on her thigh to try to calm her down, but she batted my hand away. John called just then, as he couldn't see us behind him on the road.

"Stop farting around and get on the road," John said, then hung up. I pressed the phone silent and put it in the ashtray.

"We've got to go," I said to the driver's side window, not wanting to confront Karen directly.

"Fine, then go," Karen said.

We drove over the hill and then through Daggett and up a dirt road that was barely more than a logging track, grass running down the center, a road kept open mostly by farmers for easier access to their rented fields. We drove past a gas well about fifty feet off the road. The eyesores were popping up everywhere now. This portion of the road had been blacktopped two or three times since the well went in. Those heavy gas trucks ruined the roads in a month or two. I was glad to get back onto the paved road. Karen said nothing through the whole trip. I kept expecting John to buzz my phone again and change the plan or bitch at me, but he didn't.

"I'm not going to jail for you," Karen said. She opened the glove compartment and pulled out a bag of pills. "What are these?" she asked.

"Adderall, I think," I answered, watching out of the corner of my eye as she dropped two pills and a half bottle of warm water in two swallows.

"Oh that's smart," I said. "I need you buzzing around like a freak while John and I do this."

"Be real," Karen said. "Can you even see John anymore?" I looked in the rearview and his new blue truck was nowhere to be seen.

"Fuck," I said.

"Told you," Karen said. "He's going to make you do it so he can blame you if something goes wrong."

"No, he won't."

"God, your dad is right. What a fucking child you are." The Adderall didn't take long to kick in. She drummed her fingers on the door and her face twitched every few seconds. She had the drug tolerance of a toddler.

"Give me a couple Adderall. At least we'll be even Stephen then." She snorted but handed me the bag. We were coming up on Coryland Road now, within five minutes of the crossroads and ten from the Proustman farm. I parked on the crossroad and flipped open the cylinder of the .357. I'd have five shots if I needed them.

"This is going to be awful," Karen said. "You better take me to a nice restaurant tonight. In Williamsport."

"Whatever," I said. "See, there's John now," motioning at the cloud of dust. Karen rolled the window up quickly.

"That's not John, that's Rocky Brewster's Big Red," she said. Sure enough it was.

"Fuck this," I said. "I'm not going to do it if John's not with us." The Adderall had kicked in and I was considering diverse and panicked ways of getting out when John tooled up on my left.

He powered down his window. "Everybody with the program?" he said. "How about you, sweet pea?" Karen flipped him off then crossed her arms over her chest. "I guess that's fine if you're with it, Jimmy."

"Chillin' like a villain, son," I said, sounding more confident than I was.

"We'll see," John said. "Stick that pistol in your pants, Jimmy. I got my own evener right here." He held up what looked like a .45 M1911, but shiny and chrome. "It's a Kimber," he said. "One thousand dollars' worth of stopping power and bust-your-ass." I responded by taking off down the road. John fell in fifty feet behind me.

"I am so dead. If my dad ever, ever finds out about tonight you're toast," Karen said. "And before you say it, I'm sure as hell not going to be the one that tells him."

The Proustman farm had the house and a utility barn on one side of the road and a barn plus another outbuilding on the other side of the road. One of them was inside milking, and that was the one we needed to brace. We parked up the road so they couldn't see our trucks. We all got out and I pointed over by the house and there was the red truck from the fairgrounds, elevated suspension and oversized wheels, everything the new farm boy needs.

"Told you," I said.

"Let's get this done," John said, hitching his drawers up. I could see the gun in his pants just like the Proustman boys would. At least I'd pulled my shirt over the butt of the .357.

"You can stay back if you want," I said to Karen.

"No, she can't," John said. "We may need her as a witness to say the Proustmans shot first." He looked sharply at Karen to impress his meaning, I guess.

"In it to win it," she said.

I opened the milkhouse door, and Walker Proustman hit me on the jaw with a fencepost. I staggered back and knocked over Karen, who swore at me before she'd even hit the ground. John caught the fencepost in his hands and wrestled it away from Walker, who was kicking and punching like a lunatic before his cowboy boot heel stuck on a fault in the concrete floor and sent him ass over teakettle.

"Where's the rest of my money, you little shit?" John said, holding the .45 on him. I still couldn't quite operate, but I did stagger up to my feet at least, leaning on Karen, who was humming the word *fuck* repeatedly in my ear.

"It's in the truck," he said. "Unless Jerry or Jeff got to it. I been milking cows." Walker rubbed his face where John had hit him with the .45.

"No you haven't," is what I tried to say, but nothing like that came out of my mouth. Then Jeff Walker came out of the barn side of the milk house with what I hoped wasn't a shotgun. He boomed off a shot which crumpled John's gun hand and made him drop the .45. While I stood gaping at Jeff, Karen grabbed the pistol out of my pants and pointed it at Jeff like she'd done it every day of her life. She closed one eye and shot Jeff twice in the chest. He pitched over where he stood and dropped the shotgun. Walker made a move toward it but Karen blasted him once in the head, spreading brain matter and skull fragments all over the cooling tank. Then it was silent. I still couldn't talk or hear, but just looked at Karen, her face and chin spattered with Walker Proustman's blood.

"Well, she's a keeper," John said. He handed Karen a rag from a bucket next to the sink. She wiped the grip and the barrel and put the gun down on the floor.

"We done here?" she said, wiping off her face with another rag.

"I guess so," I said. My jaw hurt like fire.

"Karen, why don't you run over to that truck and get my money?" John said. Karen ran across the road in that short hoppy stride some girls had, reached in the truck and got the bag. As we jogged up the road to the trucks, she opened the bag.

"Lookie lookie," Karen said, and lifted out two packages of hundreds. "The pot is there too!"

"What a day," John said. "Let's go home. I'll see you lovebirds in the morning. Both of you."

"Both of us," I said.

"Both of you," John repeated. He gave Karen a few hundreds for her trouble, and she bandaged up his arm and wrist with his T-shirt. He drove up the hill and was gone. Jeff Walker didn't catch him with too many BBs, then.

As for Karen and I, that night we went to the only Japanese place we could find in Williamsport. I sipped miso soup out of a straw trying to ignore my missing teeth while she ordered a bunch of exotic shit I'd never eat myself and paid for it out of the money John had given her. Later that night we messed around a bit and in the dark of the moon she proposed to me. I said yes. She's a keeper.

BIG DADDY

1995, Splitsville, PA, Pocono Mountains

Stacy Rich kept a box cutter in her uniform pocket because of men just like Big Daddy. The more she learned about him, the more scared she got. Respect. He had it. Big Daddy's meaty fingers kept shoving into everything illegal she tried to do. Even in her new straight job, housekeeping at Buckingham Honeymoon Resorts, Big Daddy's considerable reputation kept her from making a dishonest buck for fear of raising his legendary ire. The last person who'd done so had ended up, throat slit and floating at the edge of the lake at the Tobyhanna Army Depot. Stacy knew something about the kind of men who did those gigs, saw them in their matching tracksuits and ordinary-guy clothes. They looked like they had jobs, not gangbangers or men just out of the joint not even trying to go straight. They dressed nice and normal, but their eyes were off, as dead as a bug's. She'd spent her life around men like them and knew them well.

She'd also heard from her friend Pablo that Big Daddy needed someone trustworthy, someone rock-solid, but hard. Unable to be fucked with. Stacy needed a steady, unflashy source of secondary cash, which, for an ex-con, didn't come easily. Her daughter, Sylvia, was special needs, and even the cheap pre-school she was in cost all the money Stacy made and most of the pittance her baby's father, Alfred, paid in support. This housekeeping gig was the best legal she'd been able to haggle, but it didn't take her long to figure out how shit went down, and she kept her ear to the ground waiting for the right opportunity to present itself.

In the meantime, Stacy smiled and yessired the guests till she felt like her eyes might pop out. Day after day, cleaning the filthy pigs' rooms. Champagne bottles floating in the pool, cum in the saunas, boob prints on the glass of the pool room, puke in the trash cans. Video cameras pointing at the round beds where they all did their honeymoon business. Stacy had seen it all, but even the laundered sheets and towels that came in off the truck every morning in six-foot-tall blue plastic bins had the stink of Big Daddy on them. He controlled nearly everything that involved money or illegal trade in the Poconos, from the shores of Lake Wallenpaupack to the streets of East Stroudsburg, to the city and back. She didn't even know what he looked like. He was just there, slinking along I-80 from the city every day like a great goddamned nightmare.

Stacy waited in the laundry area with the other housekeepers, plus a houseman per crew waiting for room assignments. "Stacy, take Chaz and Phyllis and do the Lakeside Chalets. Hustle and you can get to the

Sweetheart Towers by noon," Edna, head of house-keeping, said. Chaz, a lanky guy with a little hipster beard, grabbed a vacuum and a box of trash can liners. Phyllis sighed, still hungover from last night's after-work stint at the Pocono Gardens, the local water-ing hole frequented by most of the housekeeping and maintenance staff. Stacy grabbed the keys to the num-ber one truck and took off out the door. She didn't like anyone else to drive, not since Chaz had let the truck out of gear and let it ride into the shallows of the lake.

Phyllis leaned over, pressing her boobs into Stacy's shoulder, and laid on the horn as they passed the maintenance building and the men lounging about at the front of the garage. "I got laid last night and I don't give a fuck," Phyllis yelled out the window.

"Christ, you stink," Stacy said.

"I told you I don't give a fuck," Phyllis said. "If I wasn't hammered still, I'd give those guys an eyeful."

"Do it," Chaz said.

"White people are fucking weird," Stacy said, tak-ing the curve toward the Lakeside Chalets at a high rate of speed, bouncing packets of burgundy towels against the wall of the built-up truck. Chaz nod-ded as if he knew exactly what Stacy meant. White-ass poser motherfucker. He'd asked Stacy one day if she wanted some cocaine. No big deal. Kept it in his lunch pail like a cheese sandwich, and together they'd snorted lines off the back of a rose-colored toilet in the Sweetheart Towers and renewed their scrubbing of the whirlpool tub with vigor. Ever since then, he'd wink at her occasionally like they were part of some secret club of outlaws. He knew she'd been in jail, but not what for, and Stacy preferred to keep it that way. Better for everyone, especially Sylvia, if no one knew about her past.

"Damn right I'm weird," Phyllis said. She leaned out the window again and yelled at a group of ducks waddling across the road to the lake. "Waah! I don't give a fuck!" Stacy shook her head at Chaz, who laughed and drummed his hand against the side of the towel rack to a tune only he could hear.

* * *

This particular tub had a ring of grime, and it took all of Stacy's two-handed strength to get it off. "I don't know what these people are doing in here," she said, "but this tub is dog-filthy."

"They're not supposed to have dogs," Phyllis said, sweating freely as she and Chaz changed the round bed with rectangular sheets.

"I don't know what all this is, but it comes off like gravel." Stacy leaned back on her calves from inside the tub.

"Maybe maintenance needs to take care of this one," Phyllis said.

"You just want Gary to show up and save the day for you," Stacy said.

"Ooh, Gary," Chaz said from the other side of the bed.

"Fuck off," Phyllis said. "Gary's not on today." She grinned, showing off her one silver tooth. "And that sucker better not show up today after the way he left me last night."

"Here we go," Stacy said.

"I heard Charley got fired yesterday," Chaz said. Stacy and Phyllis both stopped what they were doing. How did this cat always have the news, Stacy wondered?

"Says who?" Phyllis said.

"I heard it when I dropped off towels at the pool," Chaz said. "Somebody I don't know, a cheese, was talking to Johnno."

"Well, if it was a big cheese," Phyllis began. Stacy laughed. Phyllis took an inordinate amount of pride in knowing who would get canned before it ever showed up in regular gossip, especially if it had to do with housekeeping or maintenance, which Charley had joined at the beginning of the summer. Stacy tried to imagine the bags of cocaine in his greasy automotive fingers, but couldn't. Chaz, though, had to get the drugs from somewhere.

"It was Big Daddy," Chaz said.

"You are out your goddamned mind," Stacy said. "That man would never show up in a place like this." The truth was somewhere in between. He'd show up, but it'd never be so openly, getting rid of the ready connection to drugs many of the resort's guests wanted during their honeymoons and vacations. At least a couple housemen and maintenance men made good tip money bringing alcohol and small-time drugs, pot and cocaine, in to the people who needed it.

"Charley got his coke from somewhere," Chaz said.

"Shit. Wait till lunch. I'll find out what's going on," Phyllis said. "Big Daddy my ass."

Stacy nodded to Chaz. "You think you can fish those magnums of champagne out the shower before we go?" Chaz sighed, but leaned over and picked the bottles out of the tiled stall. He also picked up a can of soda heaped over with cigarette ash, dumping some onto the floor accidentally. He turned the water on and rinsed it away without soaping it down.

The crew only split eight dollars per chalet per crew, plus minimum wage. You could make out pretty well if you got assigned somewhere else, to the Sweetheart Towers or the special time-share condos the resort set up on the far end of the lake. There were only ten or twelve of these cheap-rate chalets, and they took a long time to clean, so nobody made any real money there. It was a rigged system. The favorite group got the good rooms, and Stacy's crew always ended up on the Lakeside Chalets and Roadside Villas. If they hustled, though, they could clear the whole lake and head over to the Sweetheart Towers, where the real money and the tips were.

Stacy grabbed the tied garbage bag and tossed it over her shoulder as they exited the room. This Charley thing might have created an opening for her, but she fingered the box cutter in her pocket as she walked to the next chalet and opened the door from her ring of keys. Careful, was the word.

* * *

"So. The deal is Gary said that Charley was supposed to do a brake job on the old lady's car and he didn't do it in time." Phyllis grunted and waved her sandwich. "So that's why he got let go."

"Uh-huh," Chaz said, sneaking a quick look at Stacy. The old lady owned the resort, and often had her car worked on by the maintenance crew, just as she had the housekeeping crew clean her house.

"Don't look at me," Stacy said. "I don't know what the fuck is up with anything around here. Here one day, gone the next." Five minutes later she excused herself to the bathroom and the pay phone. One quarter got her the man she wanted.

"Pablo," a guttural voice said.

"Pablo. This is Stacy. You know which one. I hear you got an opening." Five minutes later she had a meeting set up for 6:30 in the McDonald's parking lot in East Stroudsburg. She whistled between her teeth as she walked back into the laundry room that also served as the break room.

"That was the best piss she ever took," Phyllis said. Stacy smiled and flipped her the bird.

"After lunch, you guys take the Towers," Edna said, her hand over the receiver of the phone.

"Yeah, ladies, once in a lifetime" Stacy said. She stood and wadded up her lunch bag and tossed it in the trash. "Let's get this moneymaker rolling."

* * *

By 3:00 p.m. they'd cleared out most of the Sweetheart Towers and wouldn't get any more assignments for the day. They slowed down for a couple cigarette breaks, sitting just outside the truck on the telephone pole pilings that served as rustic-looking fences, door to Tower 303 gaping open. Chaz and Phyllis smoked Marlboro Reds, and Stacy took one even though she didn't smoke anymore. Chaz looked preoccupied, so Stacy hit him up. "What's up with you, Chaz? You got a girl somewhere in Mount Pocono I know. Sharon?"

"I got a couple, if you really want to know," Chaz said. "But the lady you're referring to lives in Reeders."

"Way out in the damned boonies," Stacy said, tapping her cigarette into the gravel road.

"Sharon's a good girl," Chaz said with a lazy smile.

"I'll bet," Phyllis said.

"I only date good girls," Chaz said.

"Is that what they call it now?" Phyllis said. Stacy laughed.

"They still call it dating, yes," Chaz said. Just then the phone in 303 began to ring, and Chaz took long, loping strides inside to answer it.

"She tracked us down," Phyllis said.

"Take one damned break," Stacy said, hiking herself to her feet and crushing her cigarette under her sneaker. "They catch you." She heard Chaz's voice risen in a question, and he walked out and waved.

"Edna says there's an early checkout in the condos. We need to turn it around now."

"All right, back on the clock," Stacy said, clapping her hands. The condos paid a lot more than any other units. They'd take the full hour and a half to clean it, too, but her mind was already on her meeting with Big

Daddy's man. As she scrubbed the toilets and hustled sheets onto the beds, she thought of every which way the meeting could go down, what she would say, how she would say it, rehearsing in her mind when to act hard and when to act a little aloof. If she could take over Charley's action like she wanted, she could make a lot of money very fast, especially as they were coming into the honeymoon season. The thought of it gave her a strange thrill she hadn't felt in a long time, as well as a little sliver of doubt in the back of her mind. She had a good thing here, made enough money to get by. But she wanted more, like everybody wanted more, and a little something on the side for Sylvia and her would be nice. She was on her way up, and out, she told herself as she clocked out at the end of the day, just a little late, like a good girl—4:45 exact. Time to get some food and pick up Sylvia from her mother's.

* * *

Route 611 at 5:00 p.m. was bumper-to-bumper with people trying to get back on 80 after stomping up and down the Poconos looking for horseback riding and water parks and nice restaurants, whatever the fuck these people did with their time after work and after their perfect children came home. Stacy timed her gas pedal to the brake in front of her and fumed. At this rate she wouldn't get there in time to eat anything, or more importantly, get Sylvia something to eat.

Sylvia sat in the back seat playing with a plastic pony and drooling. At three she was slow to use the potty, slow to use words, but her big brown eyes spoke volumes, and Stacy felt just a tick of guilt at what she was taking her daughter into, but it couldn't be helped.

If she asked her mother to watch her for even fifteen minutes extra, her mother would get on her something fierce. Who you seeing? What you doing? Did you work late? Why can't you pick your daughter up on time? On and on it would go, and Stacy, given the free childcare, would take it the same way she took special requests at the resort: teeth clenched behind a closed-mouth smile.

She beat time against the insistent tick of her blinker, making the right into the Mickey D's parking lot. At the end of the lot, behind the drive-through, she saw a powder-blue Mercedes and next to it a small black old-school VW bug. Inside the bug, she saw her man Pablo next to a huge long-haired white man in a tank shirt who slung over the entire passenger side. When he shifted, the entire car rocked. Stacy breathed once deeply and first drove through the window and got Sylvia a Happy Meal. She handed it to her over the back seat, then drove around and backed into the slot the Mercedes had vacated, so the driver's side abutted the person she could only assume was Big Daddy. The things you couldn't guess about a person. She'd always thought he was named after the movie the way these guys named themselves. Never assume: it was a lesson she thought she'd learned already.

She rolled her window down, but the big man's only opened a crack. He had to rear back in his seat to angle the window the rest of the way down, and it took all his fat breath to do it. "You're Stacy." Stacy nodded, and the big man looked at Pablo and nodded, and then spoke again in a high, reedy voice. "You know who I am," the man said. Stacy nodded again, not trusting her voice. The car, the man, had an odor about him like patchouli and pot and something else deep under it, a body smell like nothing she'd ever smelled. And it came all the way out the window and into her car. "You know I take no shit. You know the resort is big business for me during the summer especially. I need an ear to the ground. Pablo knows you and says you're solid. You talk only to Pablo. You talk to someone else about me you get fired. You breathe wrong and my name is on your breath, you get fired."

He glanced at the rear seat. At Sylvia. He breathed out noisily. "No reason for anything to get more ugly. Call Pablo and check in with him periodically." He reared back in the seat again and dug out a wallet attached to a chain and handed her twenty bucks. "I like your daughter," he said. "Cute." Stacy glanced at Pablo, eyes narrowed. Pablo held his hands up in the universal gesture *I don't know* and pulled carefully out of the lot, across traffic and back up 611. Stacy looked in the rearview at Sylvia and caught a trickle of sweat leaning down her temple.

"Mama," Sylvia said, and threw the pony at the back of Stacy's head and giggled. So it was on. She ran the drive-through again and got them both sundaes.

* * *

Six days later, Stacy happened to be in the resort restaurant dropping off tablecloths and heard Johnno—there he was again, running his mouth; was he one of Daddy's or just a gossip?—talking about Charley. "Sure was a good mechanic. It was a shame to lose him because of the old lady." Stacy made a mental note. She managed to be around in all the high-traffic areas to catch up on who was sleeping with who, which maintenance man had an alcohol problem, and most of all, who Chaz was supplying. He thought he was quiet about it, he thought he was slick, but poser beard-boy spent a whole lot of time delivering extra towels and pillows to people who requested them when everyone in housekeeping hated to make those runs. People in the expensive rooms never tipped well, and people in the cheap suites felt entitled. Stacy called Pablo with the information she'd gathered, and at the end of the day Sylvia's Happy Meal had an extra hundred bucks tucked into the nugget basket. Easiest money she'd ever made, and all she had to do was pay attention.

The next day she made a call to Pablo and he told her to come by the McDonald's now.

"I'm in the middle of my shift," she said.

"Daddy wants to see you," Pablo said. "He ain't take kindly to no." Stacy hung up the phone and fingered the box cutter in her smock pocket.

"Look at her. Still the best shit she ever took," Phyllis cackled. Stacy snorted and went right to Edna, made up a song and dance about how her kid was sick. It wasn't the first time she'd used that excuse, and sometimes it was even true. Edna nodded at her and went back to her phone. Stacy left, stripping off her smock as she went. "Where the fuck does she get off?" she heard Phyllis say as she left. Stacy banged the door shut on her calf in her quick desire to get into the car, and swore. This better be motherfucking important.

Lunchtime at the McDonald's crowded her like nothing since prison. People in line getting their value meals and king-sized sodas. "Go large," she heard one young man say. "I'm a go large on that one and get me a twenty-pack of nuggets." Just like last time, Daddy waited in the VW bug, leaning to the side, whether from his size or the weight of his patchouli smell she didn't know. He rolled down his window and a blast of cold air hit her in the face.

"Don't lean in on me like that," Daddy said, wheezing.

"What do you want?"

"Easy, tiger," Daddy said. Pablo kept his eyes straight ahead and expressionless, hands on the wheel. "Chaz is short. By like two large. No product to back up his claims. I need him taken care of."

"Back the truck up right fucking now," Stacy said, banging her palms on the window sill and standing up. "What did you say to me?"

"You heard me. He won't expect it from you. Pablo says you got the heart of a lion."

"How the fuck am I supposed to do this? Why?" Pablo whipped the Mexican blanket off the seat. Sylvia was there, tied up and gagged. She saw her mother and tried to scream.

"Now you know why. The how is up to you. You're a smart bitch. Figure it out. I'll let her go, and give you a nice round figure, say a grand."

"How the hell am I gonna do this?"

"Tie-Dye Dave's, in the parking lot. You can catch him there." Stacy looked from side to side, fear sweat trickling down her armpits.

"Don't you hurt her. Motherfucker I will break yo ass."

"That's the spirit. Tonight at nine he'll be at Dave's. You can nail him there." Daddy leaned out the window. "I want you to tell him it came from me." Stacy nodded. It was all she could do not to scream. "Now go back to work. Play it cool, and she'll be just fine." Daddy laid one meaty hand on top of the blanket, and Stacy blanched.

* * *

At 8:30 Stacy was at the head shop, Tie-Dye Dave's, and there was no one there on a weeknight. A Grateful Dead bootleg played on the overhead as she fiddled around, buying a tie-dyed onesie for Sylvia and looking at the hookahs and pipes laid out behind a glass case, dream catchers and God's eyes hanging from the rafters with strings of beads, and Phish tour T-shirts. Dave himself even made her a paper flower, which she grimaced at as she took it from his hands and paid for her purchases with a limp twenty-dollar bill. Outside she waited for Chaz to show. Fifteen minutes later he pulled up beside her. She had the hood of her car open and looked inside as if searching for something.

"What's up, Stacy? Car trouble?" Chas slid easily out from his car and looked inside her hood. "Can't get it started?" She swore to a god she didn't believe in and slashed his right hamstring with her box-cutter. He yelped and went down, clutching at his leg, and she slammed her knee into the side of his head, bouncing it off the car with a dull thud. Woozy, she picked him up and dragged him into his still-open car door, halfway through, his eyes unfocused and blood dripping out of his ear. Then she laid his neck open to the bone with her boxcutter, barely avoiding the blood that swooped down his throat like a rash. He gagged once. "It comes from Daddy," she whispered, then the light left his eyes. She pushed him the rest of the way into his car and dropped the box-cutter into her pocket and drove off into the empty night sky.

* * *

The news at eleven held all the talk of a vicious killer in the midst of it: the honeymoon capital. Pocono Slasher, said the news ticker. Rumored Drug Arrest for Murder Victim. Stacy sat with a hyperventilating Sylvia, soothing her with chicken nuggets she didn't want and a bottle she did, even at three years old. Through it all, Stacy kept her mind off what she'd done with a bump of cocaine. For her baby, anything seemed possible, and right. Tomorrow she might slash that big bitch Phyllis, just for her mouth, but eventually somewhere down the road, her blade and Big Daddy's throat. She knew it. It made her feel warm inside, and eventually Sylvia stopped her labored breathing and went to sleep, and still Stacy fingered the blade and thought of laying open Big Daddy's throat the way he deserved. She laid Sylvia down gently on the couch and lined up two fat ones and took them down one nostril, then the other. Big Daddy, the no-count son of a bitch, would pay.

AMPERSAND

Sissy had a snake coiled at the base of her spine. It wasn't your typical asshat. Darker in color, bloody orange and that blue you only find in tattoos. I had only met her the hour before but we were getting along. She bought me a beer and I bought her several beers and I watched her purse when she went to the ladies', which was when I noticed the snake. My buddy Ray noticed me noticing. He had introduced us. Sissy worked with him at the restaurant. Ray leaned over and yelled in my ear.

"She's something."

"Yep." I couldn't quite see her now, just the top of her head as she wound her way through the bar.

"I figure she'd be good for you."

"So you said." I wondered what exactly it was about me that made her good for me. I hadn't known Ray all that long either. It had been a couple months now and he had already insinuated himself into a role in my life.

I didn't have much else going on since Ellie took the kids and split. Ray wanted to hook me up.

"She might be able to get you on part-time at the plant, too. Here she comes now. Look alive, Jared." Ray pushed his chair back and went to the bar. I tried to relax my hands so I wouldn't look so tense. Nothing will turn a woman off faster than desperation. I'd been doing odd jobs and carpentry for a couple months now, and things were tight.

"Hello again," Sissy said as she sat down. She'd fiddled with her hair and put on some perfume. She was the best-looking woman I'd ever smelled.

"Hi," I said. Ray hadn't come back to the table yet.

"Let's just go somewhere," she said. "Don't you think it's so noisy in here?" I couldn't quite tell if she wanted to go or if she wanted to *go*. You know. It'd been a long time since I'd done anything like this.

"All right," I said. "Let me talk to Ray, and we'll go." I held out her coat for her, and then went up to Ray.

"Hey, buddy," I said. "We're going to go somewhere." Ray nodded and unwrapped his fist from his bottle long enough to pat me on the arm.

"Get 'er done, my frien'." His hand was heavy.

"OK, Ray. OK." I turned back to the table and Sissy had already left. I walked out into the parking lot, gravel crunching under my feet. Sissy sat on the hood of my Corolla smoking.

"Ray's a sweetie," she said, and blew her smoke out into the night. I could see the night unfolding in front

of me in angles. I would follow the straight line until I hit a wall, then change direction, then change direction again and again till all the moves that seemed
right fuck me back to the beginning of whatever this
thing would turn out to be.

"Ray said you might make a call for me."

"Yeah?" She flicked her knee with one stiff finger. "He
said you were looking." She stubbed out her cigarette
with the toe of her boot. "Is that why we're out here,
Jared?"

"No."

"Then why?" She pushed her hands into her pockets.

"I liked talking with you in there. You smell as good as
any woman I've ever—"

"Stop that now."

"What?"

"You don't have to do this. I'll place a call in to Hunt-
ley, the supervisor. You don't need to do whatever
you're planning on doing."

"Well I want to." I didn't want chance to run away
from me. I didn't know how many more would come.

"If you really want to, then." We drove back to my
place, her following me, me imagining her hand on
my thigh, and I watched her walk into the house as if
she knew right where to go, and what to do when she
got there. That made one of us.

Sissy came in from the bathroom wearing herself.
Light eggshell skin and dark nipples like stars against

a sheet. She came over to me and held my hands, and she put them around her and I felt the knobs of her shoulder blades under my palms. Then she led me into the bedroom, and I didn't have to worry about what I was supposed to do anymore.

I woke up with her hair spread over my arm and pillow. The mist rose up from the pond out beyond my open bedroom window, and I heard the ducks out there rustling around and quacking. I kept them under an old car hood. Occasionally they wandered out into the road and got themselves killed, but I was surprisingly free from weasels, who normally got to the ducks, if anything did. I wondered if I dared to shift my arm out from under her head, and I decided in one motion to do it. Sissy's head just shifted over to the pillow and sort of snuggled in. She reminded me of Ellie. That set the whole guilt machine into motion. I should have been out trying to get my wife and kids back. I shouldn't have been out at a bar where I could pick up women. I didn't know Sissy from Eve. I could hear my ex-wife talking in the back of my mind, and I wondered where she was at and what she was doing even as Sissy slept.

I got up quietly and threw on my shoes. The ducks would be wanting food, and Sissy wasn't likely to be waking up soon. I pulled a shirt over my head quickly, and I could see another tattoo on her shoulder, a bluebird. I started getting stomach sick. I had no business being where I was and doing what I was doing. Yes, it was my life, yes it had been something set up by Ray, but I had gone on through it and there was a woman in my bed now. One who had given her body to me, or who had taken what she wanted from me. Or exchanged sex for something else of value. A contact. A love. A job. None of it seemed a good fit for what we had done. I don't like sex when it's so fraught. A good word for me, a word I learned years ago from my grandpa. He said all his life he was fraught with trouble, like a song, and in truth, the only time I was ever comfortable with the old man was when I found him dead amongst the lilacs, a bee buzzing his nose. I was fourteen.

I stopped by the back door and got half a bucket of feed and stepped out to the pond. I tossed the food on the ground in front of the car hood and squatted among them for a while, liking the feel of being part of something beyond me. The ducks didn't care. I fed them, they ate and didn't worry. They'd survive without me and me without them, but I felt bad when the little shits ended up dead in the road too. I felt responsible.

The sex had been magnanimous, that was the best way I could put it. We tried hard and mostly succeeded at having a good time. I remember when she touched my lips and I disappeared inside myself for a moment or two and came back to her pleasure, if you judged by the scratches on my back. The reeds shifted in the nearby water and a frog jumped once and disappeared. Her car sat like a cat in front of my truck. Cats at night in this weather always warmed themselves against the engine block and I hoped they got out in time. Most of them did.

When I got back inside Sissy had started up the coffeepot. The eggs sat on the counter and she'd already broken a couple into a bowl. She'd gotten out the cast-iron fry pan I never used.

"Hey." She was in my T-shirt and a pair of silver panties. I hadn't even seen them last night. Didn't remember taking them off her, didn't remember a whole lot except how good it felt to have a woman near again, strange smells and all. There was a balance point between that and my old life, but I had yet to think of where it might lie.

"Hey yourself," I said.

"I don't know how you like your eggs so they're getting scrambled." She whipped them quickly into a mess of yellow, threw some milk on top and some cheese. I didn't know how old the cheese was.

"You're quick with those." I sat down and then got up and brought two plates down from the cupboard.

"I used to work at the Dixie Restaurant—you know where that is?—on the breakfast shift when I was younger." She sprayed the pan and dumped the eggs in, where they immediately sizzled. I saw one more tattoo on the side of her ankle. It said "D&N" in big block letters.

"Who's Dan?"

"Dan?"

"The tattoo."

"It's not a name, if you're worried."

"I wasn't. I just wondered."

"We're not at the place where I explain that to you, yet."

She smiled at me, a little quirk of the lips, and shifted the pan over the flame. Just then I heard the rattle of an exhaust and the crunch of gravel in the driveway. I walked out in the living room. I could see a man sitting in the driver's side, but he made no move to get out, just lit a cigarette and dangled his hand out the window. It was a big hand.

"Someone you know, Sissy?" I pulled the curtain back for her. "Something I should know?"

She said Jesus under her breath and went into the bedroom and came out half in her clothes. "It's not what you think." She sat on the couch, drew her pants on and tied her shoes quickly.

"What do I think?"

"I don't know. But I don't have time to talk to you about it right now. Donald needs me. You have your eggs."

"Donald. Huh. Am I in for an ass-kicking?" I said.

"I—you know, I can't explain this right now. I have to go. He's not my boyfriend, he's not my husband. He's just Donald." She brushed past me and then looked back, kissed her hand and put it against my cheek. "I'll see you. Tonight. Yes. Tonight. I'll call you." She swung her purse into her car and the door slammed and the vehicle took off with Donald, whoever he was, following before I could really even think about it. Behind me the eggs burnt a trail of smoke into the air. I went back and turned the burner off.

Outside the ducks were raising hell. I wondered what I was into. I wondered who Donald was. I went out to the ducks to see what was going on. The car hood had fallen off the cinder blocks I had it propped with. The ducks wandered around confused. I couldn't see any feathers or blood. They were just raising hell. I lifted the car hood up to re-prop it and got a glimpse of movement underneath. I pulled it up farther, and inside the straw with the broken eggs was a milk snake about the size of my wrist. Now, I shudder at the sight of snakes for the most part but this bad boy had to go. I stepped on his midsection and he climbed up my leg to where I could get hold of his neck and I let him curl around my arm then and carried him over to the field. I didn't want to kill him. He was probably puzzled by his day just like me. Wake up, eat a few eggs, and some monster picks you up from the breakfast table and lets you go in the field. I just didn't know what Sissy was about, and it was, for me, a hard decision when I asked myself how much I wanted to know what she was doing, what she did, who she did it with. None of which was any of my business, but I couldn't help but wonder. I wondered if she'd be back at the bar that night. Most of the factory workers went there to blow off steam so if I appeared there twice in one week the fat girls on the line would make sure everyone knew about it by the next shift.

I sat through the rest of the day watching old movies on Turner Classic Movies. I saw Robert Mitchum in one movie. He had tattoos on his knuckles and scared hell out of a family. I saw Fred and Ginger so light-footed you wanted to cry. I didn't drink one beer. I wanted to get through this day in good order to get to the bar so I could see if Sissy would be there, see what this Donald was about.

It took her about two hours to show up, but I had only had three beers in that time. I looked over my shoulder occasionally for her or for Ray but they didn't show. When she did come in she looked pretty fine, all made up like she had been the night before.

"Hi, mister," she said. I raised a finger and got her a bottle.

"If you want to start talking, I want you to know I'm ready to listen," I said.

"I just didn't have time to choose my words this morning."

"Lots of time now."

"I live with Donald to take care of him." She fiddled inside her purse for her wallet. "See here." I looked at the set of pictures she showed me. Sissy sitting next to a big dark man with huge hands. Sissy standing at a grill with his hands on her shoulders. The man, Donald, was massive. He must have been way over six feet. He dwarfed Sissy. He dwarfed me, I noticed, with not a little bit of worry. Then she showed me close-ups of his face and I could see something wasn't quite right with him. He didn't have a gene disease like some people I had seen, but something off-center in his smile. Childlike wasn't it either. You could see he was no child by his size and the hair on his hands, but looking at him was disarming. Could he be violent or would he be a gentle one? Hard to tell, in these pictures, but Sissy's cheeks flushed when she talked about him, in embarrassment or something else.

He was a friend of her brother's, she said, someone similarly afflicted as her brother but someone with no family to care for him. Sissy's family had done their Christian duty and taken him in and raised him as one of their own. I nodded through this as if I knew what that meant, but her stories of him showed I clearly didn't. When her own brother died—a charged moment for her—then her mom and pop died, she simply took over Donald's care. He required less and less when he got older, and he had held down a job for the last five years as a janitor at the local middle school. He'd never live on his own, never pay his own bills, but he had a pretty good life, she'd said. Better than an institution would have given him.

"You got kids?" I asked.

"No. Married once, but it didn't take." She put her hand on mine. "The situation turns off a lot of guys."

"I can see that," I said.

"Does it turn you off?" she said, putting her hand under her chin. The lines cleared in her face suddenly as she seemed to know what I'd say.

"I don't think so," I said, "but I probably ought to know more about it before I say for sure."

The lines returned. "That's fair."

"Does he always follow you around?" I imagined how that would feel and didn't like it.

"You have to tell him what barriers there are, what restrictions there are, and he'll observe them, mostly."

"Mostly?"

"He worries about me, just like anyone else would."
She tipped her drink back and tapped for two more. I
could see Ray at the end of the bar give me a thumbs-
up.

"I guess that's OK."

"Do you, now?" she said, cocking her head to the side.
"I'm glad it meets with your approval."

"I didn't mean—"

"It's fine, stop," Sissy said, laughing. "I know what you
meant."

"Let's go back to my place, then." I drained my beer.
"Will Donald make me nervous again?"

"I don't know," she said, wrapping her coat around her
arm. "We'll know in the morning."

"Good deal," I said.

* * *

I opened my eyes at 9:30 a.m. to the phone ringing.
Caller ID said it was Ellie. I let it ring. I went to the
bathroom to brush my teeth before Sissy woke up and
I opened the window. Outside, the trees were heavy
wet. The air smelled clean, the odor of silage and
cow shit and standing water without much drainage
notwithstanding. The ducks didn't seem to be making noise. I stretched my arms to the ceiling and back
again, and I noticed a hulking figure squatting out by
the hood of the duck den. Sissy slept as I pulled on
my jeans and last night's shirt with my down vest and
went out the back door, after setting the coffee to per-
colate. Donald stood up as I walked toward him.

"Hello, Donald." I extended my hand to him, and when we shook, his hand was soft as a baby's.

"Hi," he said, then stuck his hands in his jacket pockets.

"You like ducks?" I said.

"I like lots of wild things," Donald said. "These black ducks are pretty."

"I got those from overseas," I said. "My wife—my ex-wife—liked them a lot."

"She don't like them anymore?" Donald asked. "What's overseas mean?"

"Well, she—my wife—doesn't live with me anymore. And overseas means over the ocean. Far away."

"Uh-huh," he said, shoving his hands deeper in his pockets, and I suddenly didn't know what else to say.

"You want to feed them with me?" I said.

"Sure," Donald said, pushing back his hair so it fit under his cap better.

I walked back to the porch and slid the top off the drum I keep the duck feed in. I could hear noise from inside that meant Sissy was rousing herself.

"Just a half a jug."

"OK," Donald said. We walked back and lifted the hood of the den only to see a whole den of milk snakes now, wound around a mess of eggs whole and broken. "Oh no," Donald said. "That ain't right." He picked up the biggest snake and threw it headlong into the deep weeds. "They'll eat every eggie you got."

"Now, no need to throw them," I said. "Let's just pick them up and put them over there. They just want food and found an easy way to get it. No need to half-kill them."

"Oh, OK," Donald said. He bent down again and picked up a fistful of snakes in each hand, and took them gently over to the hayfield and let them loose at ground level.

"That's good," I said. "Maybe they'll forget where the eggs are now." The crunch of footsteps reached me as Sissy came up and put her hand on Donald's back and mine.

"We're saving snakes," Donald said happily. He waved two more snakes at Sissy, who shuddered and put her face in my shoulder as Donald walked away.

"What's with you and snakes?" I said. "What about the tattoo on your back?"

"I don't have to see that one," Sissy said and laughed. "I wouldn't have thought you'd ask me about that one and not the *D&N* one."

"While we're on the subject then, what does that stand for?" I said.

Sissy leaned against me. "It's for Donald, and for Neal, my brother. All caps to remind me of who I am and who relies on me."

"Well, where is the you in that equation?" I said. Donald had finished snake-wrangling and bent to wash his hands in the shallows of the pond.

"I guess I'm the ampersand," Sissy said, breathing out slowly against my back.

"Not always, I hope."

"For a long time now." Sissy's eyes went to Donald. "But maybe that can change."

"Maybe," I said.

Sissy separated from me and bent to the hood. "The snakes missed one." I could see the dark tat on her back again, the bright, mesmerizing blue of it. "Here, Donald," she said. Donald took the egg with a puzzled look, but then his face brightened, and he walked over to the hayfield and tossed the egg in.

"I bet those snakes find this one easier," he said. Sissy moved her smooth hand to my back and Donald diddled back and forth on his feet, looking back toward each of us quickly, then at me for a long uncomfortable silence.

"I bet they will," I said. Behind me a duck quacked as if in answer, and Donald began to laugh.

WISH FOR WINTER

Carl Stevenson drives, wishing it was winter. It's six p.m. and he's on his way home. His sweat-thick hair pastes itself to his head, relieved of the regulation company hat that he puts on every time he leaves the truck. Trees and houses sweep by. Broad lines of orange and red thread their way into the horizon, broken by patchy billows of cloud. The breeze through the open window evaporates the dampness on his forehead, cools him. Evergreen, larch, oak, and maple rise from the slopes on both sides of the road. Carl drives this route every week, and he's stopped looking at the scenery. It never changes, and now he only stops for cows.

Mosherville is still and silent at seven in the evening. Most people are cleaned and fed, watching *Wheel of Fortune*. Groups of teenagers are knotted tightly near the entrance to the First Independent Baptist Church. He wheels the truck around in as tight a circle as its size will allow and pulls into the parking lot. Carl parks and dusts the gauges off with a rag. The church youth group is washing cars to raise money. They laugh at some joke as Carl walks up the hill, ignoring their shouted offers to wash the Mack truck. Diesel fuel odors cling to his clothes. He breathes the warm air deeply, moving more quickly, as if he can outwalk the smell.

Carl's house stands at the bottom of the small hill he's climbing, right next to the creek. He thinks of it as his property, though technically his sister Barbara owns half. Her lime-green Plymouth sits ponderously in the driveway, hood gaping wide. The car is too big, too old, and too much a gas-hog, but it is all Barbara can afford. His pickup truck is gone, too. She must have driven it to work. The truck is his admitted vice, a midnight blue F-150, balloon tires and rebuilt wooden bed reinforced with steel. She never asks to drive it, she simply assumes she can, or should, since Carl hasn't yet replaced her carburetor.

The house is old and its foundation is shifting. Because of this, the concrete and pumice porch is wrecked; cracks in the floor are wide enough for chipmunks. The plastic storm sheeting on the north side of the porch is worn and cracked also. Carl wants to fix the porch, but can't. No cash or inclination, even though the house is his inheritance, his and Barbara's, and memories of his dead parents are tied up in it. They left the house to both children, rather than to the older Barbara. They've lived a snarling existence in the house since then.

Barbara's hoe and rake lean cobwebbed to the wall, and he kicks off his boots as he enters the house, placing them behind one of the chairs. The room is filled with stale, carrot-smelling air. There are remnants of carrot on the steel sink, and the canner is half-filled with dirty water. Two or three rows of cans sit on the Formica counter, covered with towels. Fuck it, Carl thinks.

* * *

Carl comes out from the bathroom toweling his hair, and he sees Barbara walk through the door. She is of average height. Long curly red hair hangs from her head in knots.

"Hi Carl. How was work?"

She sits at the table in the front room, her shoulders rounded and low.

"You didn't clean up the sink." It is an accusation, not a statement.

"Carl, the dogs are loose again," Barbara says, ignoring him.

"I'm busy. Just go catch the damn things and tie them up again. It's not that hard."

Carl squirts dish soap into the sink, picks up a plate and scrubs it with a Brillo pad. It scrapes against the china. He hears the door slam, listens to the pups' excited yapping. After ten minutes Barbara comes back in.

"Carl, take care of your own dogs."

He continues scrubbing pots, raises an eyebrow. Barbara's face glows red, and her breath comes in short, sharp puffs. She turns away from him. Her back rigid and arms crossed tightly over her breasts, she enters the bathroom.

Carl puts the dish down carefully. He can still hear the dogs. He cleans the dish scum from his hands with cold water, scouring his palms, feeling the pressure. Dead wet skin falls off in soft dabs of white. As he walks through the kitchen and out the door Barbara begins to sing in the shower, some country song about God will, but I won't.

The dogs disappear before Carl steps outside. The grass is uprooted where they've been digging at the ground. Carl untangles the chains, throws each in a different direction. The water dish is overturned. Carl squats, fills it at the faucet on the far wall of the house. His knees crack as he rises. An early moon rises pale over the peak of the barn. Tree frogs sing in the distance, and the night silence should be soothing—the noise of diesel engines finally gone—but it isn't.

He whistles through his teeth, two sharp notes, and nothing happens. Two more whistles, longer, shriller, and the dogs come running, tongues pink and long, lolling out of mouths just beginning to show adult teeth. He snaps the chain in each collar, roughs the dogs up gently. As he turns to walk into the house, they begin to cry mournful puppy barks. He half turns, looks back at them. They stop immediately, so quickly that it's funny. This little quirk catches Carl's lip, bringing a corner up in a half-grin.

"Shut up, mutts." He growls with them, baring his teeth, pushing them away, pushing them into each other. A pup runs to the back of the house, squats and raises its tail, tongue lolling contentedly. Carl is slow to rise. Barbara should be finished showering by now.

* * *

"Look. All you have to do is just once, just once take the damn garbage out, or wash the dishes," Carl says.

He clenches a broom in one hand, a dustpan in the other. He knows how stupid he looks, but he continues.

"Is it that much to ask? You push buttons all day, you come home, and you can't even push a broom around the house for a fucking half hour? Bullshit."

Barbara is silent, her face dwarfed by an orange bath towel wrapped around her head. He's never figured out how she manages her temper. She leans forward slightly. Her head is up and Carl can see her eyes for the first time in the conversation. They snap steel blue. "I have a calling, Carl. You know that."

Carl shakes the broom at her, its bristles nearly hitting her in the face. "Does God ever call you to help out, wash a dish or two?" Barbara's face is pale, and a hot pink flush climbs her neck inch by inch, like a rash.

"Forget it. Come to church with me. Maybe you'd understand." She grins and finishes drying her hair.

The anger hisses out of him like air from a slow leaky tire. It's the same argument they've had almost daily for ten or more years now, his dander up, followed by her pulling the church out as if it were a shotgun, waving it in his face. Disarming him with Jesus.

"I'm busy Wednesday." He'll actually be at Myrna's, providing she's not working. He supposes Barb's argument tactic is half the point she's into religion anyway—to stop herself from being pissed off over stupid things all the time , like he is.

Barbara smiles at him, though it's more like a flinch of the lips. "So bring her along. Don't worry. You'll have plenty of time to screw afterwards."

"Would you for once not pick on a woman you barely know?" Carl shouts after her as she disappears up the stairs. He knows she won't hear him, but it makes him feel better.

* * *

Carl grabs his truck keys from the table on his way out the door. Myrna may be off work by now. Barbara watches TV, still in her bathrobe, arms crossed and rigid. He says goodbye to her, really no more than a grunt.

"Bye, Carl." Her tone is soft.

"You're a pain in the ass," Carl says.

"You're probably right. Move out. Then you won't have to put up with it anymore, you … jerk." The word seems strangely foreign on her lips. "The problem is you can't have quality of life until I'm not here. Too bad. Say hello to the slut for me." Barbara sits back down on the sofa with a thump. A leg of the couch snaps, tilting her forward. She refuses to move, keeps her arms crossed, eyes glued to the TV, refusing even to shift position. He laughs as the screen door slams behind him.

                                * * *

Barbara left the windows on the truck open, and a
mist of dew has already stained the red velour interior. He rolls them up with a vicious crank, starts the
truck with an extension of the same motion. Driving
down the road, he thinks about Barbara, and the fact
that he can't stand how nice she is, how all the time he
spends being a prick is wasted on her. She never takes
her anger out on him past the initial outburst, simply
smiles and seems to forget. He wishes she would blow
up really good, just once. She's storing it up for some
grand scene, he's sure, and as he's thinking he has to
slam on the brakes to avoid a doe and her fawn who've
wandered into the road. Hitting the deer could run a
thousand bucks, and his insurance is already sky-high.
Once he avoids them, he has time to think. Insurance
companies can't mess with your rates in act of God
circumstances.

                                * * *

French's Family Restaurant is in the full swing of
business. Carl sees ten or fifteen cars in the parking lot
and one large John Deere tractor. He pulls in next to
the tractor and shuts off the truck. The lighting inside
is bright and cheery, a reminder that the main dining room was once the showroom for a tractor deal-
ership. Tommy Jones sits at a nearby table, and just
barely nods at him. He's known Tommy for most of
his life, even played touch football with him on the
playground every Saturday, but they haven't spoken
much since high school. After Carl's parents died on
the side of Route 328, Tommy found out and was the
first one to tell Carl. He'd had to haul Carl out from

under a car in the parking lot of the Village Tavern to give him the news, but he'd been the one, and the disgust shows on his face even now. Carl knows almost all of these men, works with some of them, but no one speaks to him.

Myrna is on the far side of the room. He watches her walk from one table to the next, watching the way her hips and thighs move under the black skirt. Her black hair is tied back in a ponytail that falls halfway down her back. Her face is slender and covered in lines, as if she's spent most of her life outside. Carl feels strange, like he's just cut in on the bride and her father at a wedding dance. He knows her attraction to him is a by-product of her limited romantic opportunities here, although he's never known her to be around any other men.

Myrna seems not to be concerned with anything, ignoring the comments from the men at the counter about the band of flowers tattooed on her ankle. She sets a sandwich plate in front of him, and he feels the quick brush of her body and her tongue licking his teeth, sees her seated across from him.

"Another hour, Carl. At least. I've got to stick around for a while. Frenchy's going apeshit about the cleanup. Wait for me." As quickly as she'd sat, she leaves.

Carl eats his sandwich in silence. The bright lights and yellow curtains contrast sharply with the blues and grays of the clothing most patrons are wearing. The dining room will clear out soon. Most of the people here are long-distance truck drivers sick of eating on the road or retired locals getting together for gossip sessions, leaving behind coffee cups filled with napkins and toothpicks and leftover lemon garnishes, overflowing ashtrays on every table. He leaves his Coke on the wet napkin. Some of the retirees are hoisting themselves from their places and shrugging into nylon jackets. Myrna is in the kitchen area, talking with Frenchy. Carl sees her hands moving, can see Frenchy leaning away from her, stepping back out of her path.

Carl is amused, knowing something of what just passed, having slept next to the woman for the past six months. Soon she's next to him, hair out of the ponytail and falling over the shoulders of a denim jacket.

Opening the door, he beckons her out. She stares at him, swinging her key ring on one finger. Carl walks out ahead of her.

"I convinced Frenchy he didn't need me."

Carl laughs and puts a hand on her shoulder, massaging it through the thin denim. They decide to return to Myrna's apartment and order pizza, watch some television.

Carl spins gravel behind him for forty feet as he pulls out behind Myrna's Jetta. Gunning the engine, she manages to grab a quarter mile before Carl can get the truck into fourth gear. Once there, he cruises up to the rear end of the car and flicks his high beams on.

In the pale rectangular light of her rear window, Carl sees her arm and fist extended to the side, middle finger outstretched.

* * *

Myrna's building feels like denim. It has a feel to it that Carl likes, although it's hard to see where Myrna fits within it. The dark hallway in her building is relieved by the thin yellow light of two overhanging light bulbs. Carl remembers telling her he'd fix the blinds.

A huge wall bookcase dominates her apartment. On the bottom shelf is a compact stereo. The shelves above are overfilled with books and magazines. The floor next to the sofa is piled armrest-high with books that take over the room. The BarcaLounger next to the bookcase seats a smaller, more organized mess of books and magazines. A small television rests on the floor next to the bookcase. It seems unnatural, with its manual antenna pointing toward the window, almost an afterthought.

Myrna throws her jacket over the back of a chair, walks into her bedroom. She says something, her voice muffled by the shirt she is pulling over her head.

"What?" Carl is already stretched out on the sofa, boots unlaced and set carefully by the door. He pulls his socks on tighter as he speaks.

Carl orders the pizza, everything but pepperoni, while flipping through *Mother Earth News*. The shower is running, thumping against the tile and the wall, water pipes hissing. Soon the noise stops. Her disembodied voice is what he hears first. She sings clear and vibrant melodies that he doesn't recognize, words like an opera singer would sing. Her voice is too full for her body. Carl expects a statuesque woman with blonde braids and quivering lips to sound like that.

Myrna comes out in cutoff sweatpants and an over-large T-shirt. She reminds him of Barbara.

"What's the matter with you?" Her hair is wet, straggling down her back. "You look like I just shit in your lap."

"Nothing." Carl's voice hardens at the end, cutting off the question.

"Let me guess."

"Don't bother."

"What did she say this time? Did she leave the toothpaste cap off?" Myrna smiles with her eyes. It makes her look years younger.

"She don't do a goddamn thing around the house. She won't wash the—"

"Enough already. Whatever, she probably doesn't deserve it." Sighing, Myrna leans down, turns on the TV.

Carl stares at her, swings his legs off the couch and onto the floor. His feet smack against the floor, as loud as if he were wearing boots. His feet sting.

"Don't get all hyper. You're more of a tight-ass than you want to admit, especially to your sister."

"Barb hates you."

"I know. Remember, I visit occasionally?"

Carl swallows his tension. It goes down hard.

"Go get the pizza." Myrna is smiling again.

Carl breathes in, once, twice, and opens the door.

The pizza is lukewarm, heavy with tiny hard granules of pepper. Myrna chews quickly, stopping only to sip from her beer. The television is glowing, three or four teenagers wrestle with a late-night ghoul, stabbing it repeatedly, greenish dark blood dripping onto the floor. Carl imagines the zipper going up the monster's back, the two- or three-hour makeup sessions. There are no screams, and the monster never grunts. Myrna prefers to watch monster movies with the sound turned down. Carl never asks why. He's learned to adjust. He's almost learned to enjoy it the way Myrna seems to, making up his own words for the action, labeling the women with names like Karen and Donna and Cindy, Cindy who always dies first.

Carl puts his arm around Myrna, reaches under her arm and cups a breast. Without breaking her eyes from the screen she reaches up, takes his hand away, puts it in her lap.

Carl brings his arm back, cracks his knuckles against the back of the couch.

"Jesus. Cut it out." Myrna swivels her head. Her eyebrows are drawn in. "I hate it when you do that. It sounds like your fingers are breaking or something."

"Sorry."

"Now I missed it." The movie has gone to commercial. Rising from the couch, Myrna walks into the kitchen. He watches her calf muscles bunch and unroll. The refrigerator door opens, the sucking noise of the seal followed by the rattling of dishes.

"Do you want a beer?" Her voice sounds cavernous, echoing through the kitchen.

Carl considers this for a moment. "No thanks." Beer is something he's never found a taste for, its bitterness and foam unappealing. Too much like he imagines urine might taste.

"Movie's back on." Cindy is on the screen, back from the dead.

Myrna hasn't come out from the kitchen yet. This is probably a danger sign. Her moods swing quickly. She told him once after a protracted struggle over the beer he spilled in her hydrangea that she got no fulfillment from him, and he imagines his knuckle cracking has sent her over the edge of anger this time. Carl picks up the pizza carton, tosses the beer cans inside it, sets it outside the door of the apartment. Carl reaches up and puts his fingertips on the ceiling, trying to relax his sore back muscles. He hears some thumping from next door, a television turned up, overloud screams. He can't tell if it's the television or not, and it's none of his business really, so he ignores the noise and walks back into the apartment and into the kitchen.

Myrna is looking out the window. Her arms are resting on the stainless steel sink, hair falling over a shoulder. Her face is bathed in hard white light from the pole outside the window. He can see a scar on her chin that he still cannot trace, old boyfriend or childhood accident, and her earlobes stretched from the heavy brass earrings she wears. She hears him approaching, but doesn't turn around. Carl reaches under her arms, cups her breasts, feeling the stiffness there, and she turns quickly, her face inches away from his. He moves to kiss her, but stops, seeing the look on her face.

"Go home, Carl." She looks him in the eye.

"What?" Carl is shocked, not at the request, but at the tone of voice. Her voice is low and dark, like her hair.

"Go home. You're pissing me off."

"Fine." He knows better than to ask now. He'll wait a day. Give the initial mood time to pass. He throws his boots on, and without tying them, walks out.

* * *

Bright points of light shine through the windows, drilling through his head to the back of his skull. He's positioned himself this way deliberately, sleeping with his head at the foot of the bed, as he's done since childhood. The sun works as a better alarm clock than any he could buy. The floor is cold under his feet. He stretches once, lifting arms up, rotating them back and forth, feeling last night's tension in his neck still, like a bungee jumper's cord on the downward arc.

The shower is a welcome thing, even though the bathroom is tiny. Carl feels larger than life in the shower, the steam rising and billowing, like monster movies from the fifties, where the hero would come out from the mist and save the heroine. He fills the room.

This morning he can't even begin the ritual. Longish rows of dark shapes hang from the shower rod like dismembered corpses. Barbara's nylons. The toilet cover is down, and a small bottle of cherry red nail polish sits directly in the center of it. Carl can see Barbara there, almost, putting one dainty little foot onto the seat to paint her equally dainty little toes. He picks up the bottle and deposits it in the medicine cabinet, where it belongs. The nylons belong in the garbage. Carl can see the beginnings of a run in almost every one. Outside he hears Barbara stirring. Thrusting the stockings into an empty box of panty liners, he throws the whole thing into the garbage.

"Morning." Barbara's hair is a tangled mess, flat on the left side. She half-heartedly plucks at it with her fingers.

Carl grunts.

"How's the bitch?" Barbara stumps into the bathroom, throwing the words behind her as an afterthought.

"Starting off early, aren't we?" Carl says.

Carl can't hear the response Barbara gives.

The route is already blazing. Carl imagines the tops of the trees, the leaves dry and cracking as they will be in a few days. The summers keep getting hotter. The last time Carl remembers heat like this was when he'd delivered nuclear waste products from power plants to dumps in the middle eighties, just after Three Mile Island and before Chernobyl. The heat got so bad near the reactors that air conditioners were useless. He saw workers, so hot they were unable to sweat, get taken out on stretchers. The treetops shimmer like the blacktop in the parking lots in those days. He suppresses a shudder, remembering the documentaries that few took seriously, three-legged cows and radiation sickness. He got out of the business soon after that, doing long-haul routes for a local trucking company until just recently, when he began hauling milk for better pay, better benefits, and no chance of radiation poisoning. Even now, he wakes up in the morning feeling for the first signs of baldness, pink patches on the skin, stomach palpitations. The fear never leaves.

His first stop is local, the Jessup farm, where Jessup milks forty cows and keeps a coffee maker in the milk house. He's one of the new breed of farmers, college educated, almost contemptuous of what he does, referring to it as agricultural engineering. Jessup's a bit different though, willing to help a cow birth, willing to shovel shit if need be. Jessup and Carl have some things in common.

Up early, Jessup is always milked by 6:30, another rarity in the new breed of farmer. This is why Carl stops here first, killing a little time, letting the others have some time to milk their herds. He likes the small break right at the top of the morning. It gives him time to think about the day.

"How goes it?"

"Awful." Jessup's face seems more lined than usual.

"What's going on?"

"One of my best milkers got nabbed by a pack of wild dogs two nights ago. Got hung up in the fence and never had a chance. I lost five grand and a hell of a lot of moo juice."

"Call the game warden."

"Already did. Says he can't do anything about it."

Carl plucks his cap from his head, runs a hand through his hair, sets the cap down again.

"I got a solution for you."

"What's that?"

"Why don't I bring my .22-250 over around 7, 7:30? You and I could put a stop to this shit right now."

Jessup is silent.

Carl thinks that Jessup is going to accept. He doesn't understand the hesitation.

Jessup speaks over the hum of the machinery in the milk-house. "You know whose dogs they are."

"Smitty's old lady."

"That going to be a problem?" Carl knows Jessup is thinking about the possible repercussions. Smitty's wife still thought the dogs tame and harmless, when they'd been running wild and downing cows and house dogs for years.

"Don't see how. We'd be doing everyone a favor."

"Fine. See you at 7. Maybe buy a six-pack," Jessup says nervously.

"Sure. Got to get going. Got a bunch of stops yet today."

Jessup turns and walks into the dim light of the barn, lifting a hand in a slight wave.

Carl carries his coffee to the truck and pulls out, blowing the horn once in farewell.

Carl pulls back up to the Jessup farm at 6:45 in his pickup. The sky is still bright, but darkening, soon to be a bluish black. The weathervane on the peak of the barn impales a fat yellowish orange sun. In the rack behind him is the lesser of his two prides, a Remington .22-250. Beside him on the side is a box of shells. He whistles tunelessly; Jessup meets him as he nears the milkhouse. Jessup carries a rifle similar to Carl's, with an open sight instead of Carl's scope. In his right hand he carries a thermos. They nod in greeting.

"Nice night."

"The gnats are going to be hell."

"Hopefully we won't have to be out here that long." Carl cocks an eye at Jessup, who is jiggling the thermos up and down in a jerky motion.

Silent, they walk toward the canopy of trees that rise a hundred yards or so from the rear of Jessup's barn. The ground is pocked and nearly grassless. Bare patches mark the spots where Jessup places his salt licks. A small brown stream runs the length of the field, meandering in gentle curves toward the trees. Carl sees clouds of gnats already forming, stirred by the noise of their passing. Half of a rusted fuel drum is planted in the ground near the border of the tress. Carl sits. Reaching into his pocket, he brings out a long, slender stick. Lighting the tip, he tucks it into the brim of his hat. He loads the rifle with a clip, setting the remainder of the box on the ground beside him; Jessup's rifle is already loaded.

The air is still enough for Carl to hear tree frogs. The only other sound is Jessup slapping bugs off his skin. Carl is almost dozing by the time the first rustle reaches his ears. Jessup has left to put the cows in for the night.

The rustle grows in volume. Carl stills himself, barely breathing, adrenalin pumping. Slowly he turns. The dog's eyes follow him. Slowly he raises the rifle, his lips tensing, forming one straight line in the soft angles of his face. The dog's eyes disappear, replaced by two more pairs, then another.

A long angular body appears in his sighting pattern. Carl catches the faint sound of panting, looks up from the scope and takes a moment to let his eyes adjust to the sudden wide angle. He puts his eye back to the sight, squeezes off one round, throws the bolt, shoots again, almost before the animals react to the sudden impact of the bullet. In the distance he hears a yelp, swears to himself, knowing he missed. By this time Jessup is hurrying back across the field. Carl can hear him pant, just like the dogs.

Reaching him, Jessup shines a wide ray of yellow light toward Carl. Carl points in the direction of his shot, looks down, away from the light, to reload. Jessup's light reveals a black and tan down and still. A few feet away another dog is panting laboriously, coat covered in dark. Carl walks to him, shoots him in the head. The dog's rear leg twitches, even after death, pawing its shoulder for fleas. He's glad his pups are too young yet to be chasing things around.

"Well, that's two, anyway. Won't be bothering your heifers tonight."

"Yeah, tonight."

"Just have to keep doing this for a few nights, you know, narrow them down, they have less a chance of pulling your cows down again."

"Yeah."

Jessup is looking into the woods, eyes searching the dark, for more dogs, Carl thinks.

"What's the matter?"

"That dog belongs to Knappy down the road."

"He should have kept him penned up."

"That's his coon dog. He paid good cash for that thing. Now you shot him."

Carl draws in a sharp breath. "How much are your cows worth again, Jessup?" He slams the clip into its recess. "How much money did you get for that last cow? Five, ten grand? He can find another dog."

"You're probably right." His voice falters a bit in mid-sentence. Carl can see the indecision in Jessup's face, the regret.

"Look, Jessup. It's simple. Your cows are worth more than his fucking black and tan. Don't worry about it."

"Absolutely." Jessup is unconvinced.

They walk silently, but twigs crack underfoot every ten or fifteen steps, startling them. Carl follows the weaving band of light in Jessup's hand, taking care in placing his feet. Jessup is not so careful. He stares straight ahead, barely concerned with the light.

"Guess I'll see you around the next run." Carl doesn't care about the response. He feels as if he's just saying it for the effect, to tell Jessup that nothing changes for him, dead dog, cow-killer, or cow-hound.

"Sure." Jessup's eyelid twitches. Carl notices this for the first time and wonders why he has never noticed this before. Jessup shouldn't be that jumpy.

"All right then." Carl puts the rifle in the truck rack and jumps into the cab. Jessup is reconnected now, looking at Carl intently.

"See you later. Thanks."

"No problem," Carl yells over the roar of the engine, popping the clutch and hitting the gas at the same time, leaving Jessup in a cloud of dust and manure.

Carl speeds on the back roads, watching the sky, his peripheral vision and reflexes responsible for guiding the truck. The moon is high, and no other stars are visible. Heavy cloud cover billows blue-white, curling and swaying over the moon. He brakes momentarily, pauses in front of his house. Seeing all the lights on, he hits the gas again. Seconds later he is pulling onto the cracked cement in front of Myrna's apartment building. He can see light through the tiny crack in the curtains covering the window. He twists the keys in the ignition, drums his fingers against the steering wheel. The curtains open, but no one is at the window. Opening the door, he slides out from the cab and falls softly to the cement. As he reaches the top step, he sees that Myrna's door is open already. Through the rectangle of light, he can see Myrna, sitting on the floor, a man leaning over her, his hands on her shoulders. He imagines that Myrna's eyes are closed even though he can barely see her at all, and blood bursts in his head, a deep, sharp glass-breaking howl of hurt that begins at the bottom of his neck and suffuses his face, his entire head, now a gigantic knot of pain.

He runs down the stairs, his boots clomping loudly, every step exacerbating the swollen-headed anger. Carl pictures her screaming his name, but he is already out the door and into the truck, and there's no noise from her apartment, or even any sign that she's noticed him. Behind the seat is a bottle of cheap bourbon, bought this afternoon in anticipation of this very scene. Myrna is his woman, but only in outward appearances, since apparently she's unfulfilled by Carl. She knew he would be there to apologize, and she brought up another man, to make sure he saw her with someone else.

Carl drinks from the bottle, and it burns. He drives home, steering with his knee, bottle in his left hand. Drunkenness seems the only way to ease his pain, at least for the moment, but he has to drive in the morning. He takes two strong pulls, caps the bottle, and puts it back under the seat. A hangover won't do him any good.

* * *

In the morning, the sun in the clouds above seems like a swollen eye to Carl, red and pulsing with heat. He pulls the truck out of the church parking lot at twenty-five miles an hour, the engine roaring. The cool morning breeze through the opened window makes a soundless and momentary brush against his unshaven cheek. He runs one hand through his hair, feels the roots pull against the pressure of his hand. Drinking never does this. Staying out all night coon-hunting doesn't cause this. It is, as always, women—either Barbara or Myrna. Carl thinks he should be used to it. His tongue seems thick and furred, and his throat is dry, and because Barbara didn't buy coffee, there's nothing but leaded well water to drink.

* * *

Jessup's farm passes by in a blur of green and gray. There will be no coffee from Jessup this morning either, as it's already almost 8 a.m. and he hasn't checked in at the plant since yesterday morning. He blats the horn once. The sound shivers into his ear, sets up a rhythm that thuds against his skull.

Eastern Milk Producers plant is nearly empty at this time of the morning. Bossman Penner left a note. Carl—*take over the first five on Tiny's route*. He's already late.

The early-morning heat has dissolved into midmorning coolness, a dew of rain beginning to snake its way across the windshield. His first stop of the day will have to be the Neary farm, about ten miles from Jessup on the other side of the road. Jeff Neary is one of the people Barbara talks about in the church, the type who always makes contributions, who is always there to crank ice cream for the twice-yearly socials, who slicks back his hair and wears a suit to the morning services. He is the softball coach for his twin eight-year-old daughters and will undoubtedly coach five-year-old Jeff Junior's Little League team when the time comes. More importantly though, Neary's milking is always done by 7:30 in the morning.

The Neary farm looks well-kept, the barn freshly painted and the milk house clean and organized. Evergreens rise in rows near the stark white farmhouse, where Neary planted them years ago. Neary milks more than 150 cows and makes a lot of money. His house is big and he has a new tractor. Carl admires and dislikes him at the same time, for the fact that Neary lives on good land with Jerseys who never seem to get mastitis, and for the way his handshake is a bit too strong and his voice slightly overloud, the way commercials sound between television shows.

The driveway that leads to Neary's milk house is narrow and slopes downward. He shifts into reverse and guides the truck using only the mirrors. Carl sees the gray cinder block of the milk house as the tank approaches. He throws a quick look back toward the road to see if he'll have to move the truck for traffic, but it doesn't seem like it'll be necessary.

He sees Jeff Neary in the rearview, and his eyes are shadowed by a hat. He is yelling and pointing toward the milk house, but Carl can't hear his words over the slow rumble of the diesel. Carl thrusts his head out the window, thinking that perhaps he's drawn too close and is about to smash the tanker bumper into the gray brick when he feels a slight bump in the motion of the truck and he sees Jeff Neary Sr. fall to his knees in the mud and cow shit and reach up for his hat. Pulling it off, he reveals a bald head burnt pink on the forehead, left stark white on the top, and his face loses its expression by degrees, slowly fades into nothing.

Carl thinks it must be a rock, or one of the farm cats that haunt barns until he sees a yellow plastic wheel superimposed on the black of his rear tire. He shuts the engine down and jumps out onto the ground, and over the ticking of the engine he can hear a soft whimper. He stands in his place. The smell of cow shit is overpowering. The rain brings the smell out of the ground and he realizes the noise comes from Jeff Sr., who holds his battered John Deere hat in his hands, twisting it, the green and yellow prominent against his coveralls.

"Jesus." Jeff Sr. is barely coherent, his face twisting into a mask.

Carl stares at the truck wheel. He can't hear any noise from the rear of the truck, which doesn't concern him, somehow. It seems everything is working against his true perceptions, that he is imagining this whole incident before it has happened. His reactions are slowed, as if he were pulling his way through the swamp after raccoon, each leg held by mucky grass and deep mud.

"Jesus. Jesus Christ," Jeff Neary says.

Carl reaches over to him, grabs him by the shoulder, tries to pull him up. Neary clutches at his wrist, then forearm. He pulls Carl down in the mud with him. To gether they stare at the rear wheels of the truck, where the yellow wheel of the plastic Big Wheel has fallen off and lies on the ground, when a cry of pain creeps slowly into Carls' head. He can't tell where it is coming from, and his temples throb, and the sun climbs high in the sky now, clear and bright. The cloud cover is gone, burnt off hours ago. There is a child under the wheels of his tanker.

* * *

He remembers the questions only in retrospect: had he been drinking, was he feeling okay, could he drive the truck back to the plant. He remembers telling them (to whom, he doesn't' know, Frank Congdon the fire chief maybe) he is fine to drive, he'll go slowly, and he wonders why they don't take the truck away from him and haul him to Towanda to the county lockup. Carl feels as if he should be locked up, for his own safety, like they say on TV. He thinks psychologists should be there talking to him, telling him to be calm. Instead he has Congdon's square head in his line of vision and Jeff Neary's high, keening wail in his mind. Neary's bull tears through the fencing, overexcited by the trucks and people milling around, the ambulance screeching in and leaving as soon as the boy was on the stretcher, and Congdon leaves Carl. Congdon seems more concerned with helping to direct the bull elsewhere and fixing the fence. He's a farmer at heart, even though he pulls triple duty as fire chief and township constable.

Carl gets into the Mack and pulls it out, grinds between second and third gears, turns the wheel savagely, and loses himself promptly in the sight of sunlight in the hedgerows and the hired man for Jeff Neary chopping hay in the upper half of the field.

Carl's fields haven't been touched since his father died. The farm's become ramshackle, an open show of carelessness and laziness, of Carl's life. He could do this,

118

he realizes. He too could put seeds into the ground, watch them grow, milk Jerseys in early morning like Jeff Neary. It's not as if he's never done it. He helped his father for years, even if it was nothing more than baling hay or buying chicken feed at Longenecker's Feed Store and Kennel. He wonders fleetingly about another accident as he accelerates into the downhill side of Coryland, where the loose gravel often throws cars off the road and into the picnic tables of the township park. Carl can see the barn in his mind, and thinks in the aftermath of the morning that he ought to change what he can, to fix up the barn at least, clean up what his father left him.

He doesn't want to think about the boy, whether he'll live or not. He can only think of what he should be doing. Should he go home? Word will have spread by now, the entire county glued to their police scanners, wondering who the stupid one who hit the kid was. It wouldn't take long.

Penner has undoubtedly heard already, so Carl doesn't bother to even go in to speak with him. He tucks the keys into the visor, dumps his cap and ID on the seat, and gets out. The parking lot heat burns into his shoulders through his shirt, and he sees Penner walking toward him from the office, but turns his back, heads for his truck, ignoring Penner's shout. The farm waits and the idea of cleaning things up kick-starts him into a jog for the truck.

* * *

Carl slides back the barn door. He hasn't set a purposeful foot in here for years, since just after his parents died. He leaves the barn door bolt off generally, for the use of the farmers who he rents the fields to, but this field hasn't been planted in at least five years, since he got off the nuclear waste route. He doesn't even know where the bolt is. The old Farmall is covered in a heavy patina of dust, chaff, and silver-gray bird shit.

Carl sold off almost all of the other tools. An old pickax leans in a corner, with a gray bucket next to it. The pickax handle is gnawed, probably by barn rats who've long since fled the lifeless barn. There's a roll of bailing wire rotting underneath the tractor. Nothing else but junk in the entire barn. He looks up, startled by a flapping noise, and sees daylight through a crumble of roof beams and green tar paper shingling. Everything needs fixing. He can't even think of where to begin, where to find money to buy supplies to do it. Penner will probably make him take a leave of absence, if not fire him outright. There'll be no money coming in but Barbara's.

The tractor is the most logical place to begin. It's the most easily fixable, and the one he knows most about fixing. The starter fails to turn the motor over even once. The pulley belts are worn almost through and brittle, weakened by years of neglect. The oil and gas have congealed into lumps, by now, Carl thinks. Acid from the bird shit has eaten away the red paint, leaving the dull gray underneath. Carl can see no beginning in sight, even for this, something he has some knowledge about. He leaves the tractor, walks out, feeling the adrenaline well up. He has to do something, even if it isn't right. He considers driving into the hills, but the thought of actually putting foot to gas pedal stops him.

Clouds of crows, or maybe starlings, are gathering in the back field. Carl notices that more than a few saplings have taken roots in what used to be field, along with some low undergrowth, probably mountain laurel, mixed in with the leftover timothy and oats from past plantings, seeds that have strayed from the fold and taken root elsewhere. The forest is spreading into the field. This is something Carl can prevent.

He gets the old pickax. The watering trough near the field is still operable. The source pipe still gurgles, but the surface of the water is covered in green pond scum. The chicken house has fallen in on itself. Carl wonders how he's failed to notice how bad the place looks. He feels feverish. The saplings are actually much bigger than they looked from the barn. His father must have let some of these grow. There hadn't been enough time since his death for trees to grow to wrist-thick proportions. It gives Carl some small measure of comfort to know this, that his father had forgotten or chosen to ignore these things. Carl wonders if the old pick will break before he can get them uprooted.

He circles the first tree, looking for the taproot. Once he finds it, a thin grayish ropelike thing about the thickness of two fingers, it takes only one hit before the root tears in half, revealing greenish-white new wood. From there it's only a matter of minutes before the tree lies next to a scar of brown earth in the timothy. A cloud of dust has settled near the barn. Through it he can see Myrna's red Jetta.

He turns to another sapling, a bit larger, probably an ash, although Carl isn't sure anymore. One heaving stroke cuts through the root, and he can hear the front door of the house slam. She's coming back to apologize, Carl thinks. What perfect timing. She knows I put the Neary kid in the hospital. She knows I can't drive anywhere ever, now. Three or four more hits bring the tree down, but only partway. The taproot is still connected, and he hits it again and again, waiting for the tree to topple.

From his position, he can see the house and barn in silhouette. He sees Myrna in her black skirt and white shirt coming toward him. He imagines a snake striking at her, red punctures above the roses on her ankle, and shakes the image away. He can't imagine her bringing up their relationship problems now, how he walked out and didn't call, and she didn't either. Carl doesn't want to know who he was, this nameless head he saw through the doorway, and he knows Myrna will tell him. He watches her approach, and begins to feel the tremor, a red knot of pain in his forehead that spreads throughout his body until he shakes. He feels like he's having a seizure. He needs anything but her sympathy right now, because he will not hear her speak about being sorry, or about fault or bad timing. He needs to clear this field.

"You didn't call." Myrna crouches, pulls a strand of timothy, puts it in her mouth. Her eyes are lucid even brown. She might at least have been crying for the Neary boy, if not for him. She looks like a painting, but Carl says nothing, not trusting himself to speak yet. "I know about the Neary kid, Carl."

He isn't listening to her. He moves to another sapling, cuts the tap with a brutal swing.

"Look, what are you doing?" She throws the timothy away, comes closer, stopping just short of his swing arc.

"I'll be fine." Carl has to strain. His throat is tight. "The place looks like shit."

"Since when are you a farmer?"

"I'm cleaning the place up. Busywork. Keep me busy." Carl swings once more, and the body tremors begin again. He drops the axe. Myrna grabs his hands, and he feels their coolness on the sting in his palms and immediately pulls away from her.

"Busywork? Busy in the barn? You left the door open. This isn't going to do anything for you." She tries to grab his hands again, but Carl slaps her hands away. He can't decide if she's being sarcastic.

"I didn't see him. He was just there." Carl drops to his knees to work on a stubborn root. The rocky dirt feels hot as sun-warmed sand.

"It doesn't matter. Get up and come in." Myrna puts her hands on his shoulders. It feels as if she's pushing him down even farther.

"He went behind the truck. He's a farm kid. He should know better." Carl stops pulling, rests his hands on his knees. He knows Myrna is speaking, trying to help him, but he can't really understand. It's as if she is speaking another language. The pups bark, and the noise bites through Myrna's words. Barbara must be home from work now. He hears the shrill whine of a too-fast gear change, and Barbara stalls the truck near the barn, not bothering parking at the end of the driveway.

"Come inside, Carl." Myrna pulls at his collar, and he shrugs her off, gets up and axes another tree, which falls almost immediately.

"I'll be in when I'm finished." Twilight fell somehow while they'd been speaking, and the trees now began to cast alarming multiarmed shadows, dying sunlight reflected in odd shapes.

Myrna turns her back and walks away. Barbara is on her way to him, running almost, the timothy and weeds clearing before her weight, some of it snapping back upright. Her face is flushed, features listing sideward, almost as if she's had a stroke. Carl wonders which book will do it this time. He thinks probably New Testament, maybe one of the Gospels. Carl feels more Old Testament, or maybe Revelation, waiting for black horsemen to skewer him with a spear.

"God, Carl. I'm sorry." She's breathless, and barely squeezes the words out. Carl waits. She didn't run all the way through the fields just to say she was sorry. Biblical lessons are implicit in every situation for her. It's simply a matter of time before she finds the right one. Carl leans on the axe, looks around. He's knocked out about a third of what needs to be cleared. Dirt is everywhere, and the saplings lie in haphazard patterns. Carl estimates another three or four hours to level the trees, perhaps another hour to gather the trees into a pile and burn them. He wonders if the moon will provide him with enough light to finish the job tonight.

Barbara coughs now, her face paled to a hectic shade of pink.

"Aren't you going to say something, Carl?"

"Like what?"

"Were you drunk?"

Carl knows that she knows this isn't even remotely possible, but understands her dilemma. He doesn't understand how it could happen either.

"I'm trying not to think about it," Carl says. The urgent need to do something is gone, and his arms are heavy. They seem oversized and awkward and yet the pickax in his hands is a live wire, shocking him to action. He has a tool in his hands, and he must use it. "I'm going to finish this tonight, I think. I've got some time now. I want to do it." He hears the note of pleading in his own voice and is surprised at it.

Barbara turns from him and walks back toward the house moving slowly, as if she has troubles weighing her down. Carl's lip twitches and he feels a bead of sweat roll into his mouth. In the distance he hears Myrna's engine revving, and almost immediately she is gone, and with her leaving Carl feels something in the air go flat, to be replaced by an unreasoning chill of anger. In his time of need, she leaves him for someone else.

He leaves the twilight and the saplings behind. In the rack of the truck is the .22-250, left from Jessup's dog-shooting night. Carl knows how men act who are responsible for children's deaths. One of two things will, must happen. He knows it as one of the undeniable facts of his life thus far. He's seen adjustment made with alcohol, a slow burning trip with unpleasant memories, or with violence: John Sherman cracking his wife's temple with one fist, Martin DuBois cutting wood for ten hours straight until the chain slipped and cut his leg an inch and a half deep below the knee. Or the men who strangled coonhounds who wouldn't tree anymore, ran over barn cats deliberately, or shot themselves in the mouth. The possibilities are endless.

He unslings the rifle from its position. He is breathing hard, not from the exercise, but from the elation of decision—making a mistake, seeing its consequences, and rectifying its aftermath. Once the clip is filled he puts the rifle back. Carl jumps into the truck and heads for the Neary farm.

He pulls the truck in near the barn, where he can still see his Mack's tread pattern embossed in the mud and cow shit. He jumps out of the car with the rifle, walks ten measured and long steps, puts it to his shoulder, and squeezes a round into the driver's side door, watches as a black hole rimmed with steel appears as if by magic near the door handle. He squeezes another round off, watches it powder the window into shards.

He twinges at the loss, but feels exhilarated at the same time. He remembers feeling this way as a child when he answered correctly in Sunday school class, but he can only put words to now. It was as if this single action once performed would render obsolete all the past mistakes he regrets. He steps off from the front of the truck, fires on the radiator, shoots out the headlights, pauses to reload, plinks four rounds into the windshield where the bullets crack it into concentric spiderwebs, and sends his final round head-high through the windshield and into the plush of the driver's seat.

Full night has fallen finally, but the black tar of the road still pops up in bubbles from the heat. Carl leans the rifle over his shoulder as he walks away from the truck. Tomorrow someone will say that someone shot up Carl Stevenson's truck, and that Carl was seen strolling home with his rifle on his shoulder, looking as if he had spent the day peacefully hunting woodchucks.

* * *

The morning light shines through the dirty sheet of plastic over the windows, giving a muddy white halo to the cat, who lies directly in its path. Carl can tell it's going to be ball-busting hot, and starts up the box fan in the corner of the kitchen, which kicks in with a whir and a small dust cloud billowing out. He settles down in the rocker, which he's brought down from Barbara's room upstairs. It's the rocker his mother kept, an antique handmade something or other with a missing brace on the left side, so Carl has to sit listing to the right to keep it from crumbling. At one point Carl had nailed some scrap wood to the painted oak, but it has long since gone the way of every other task in the house. Started, with good intentions, but never touched subsequently. The Bible is on the floor next to him, creased open at Proverbs. Here he can learn all the things he shouldn't have done, and won't do in the future.

Barbara will be home at noon, having taken a short-
ened shift to come home "to help him sort through
things," but he doesn't want her to know he's read the
Bible, or even that he's picked it up with serious intent.
He decides to give it up for the day. Carl stows the
Bible in the cabinet under the sink, in the mop bucket.
Finding the perfect hiding spot, where Barbara will
never even think to look or have reason to go, brings a
tiny smile to his lips.

He decides to walk the two or three miles to the Neary
farm, knowing that he'll be able to put the truck into
neutral and coast it all the way home and into the
driveway. He shouldn't have left it there, but it's a sign
to the Nearys, perhaps better, definitely better than
showing up at the hospital to pay respects he'd already
given away. He's picked a poor time to walk anywhere,
though, with the heat and the gravel at the side of the
road skipping along and crunching under his boots,
magnifying the sounds in his head.

He knows somehow that Jeff Neary Jr. should be cold
and slabbed. He realizes that something, a whispered
wind from God that blew the boy out of his truck's
path, a shout from his father, pure dumb luck, saved
him, kept the wheel from crushing his skull. Carl can't
understand it, the way things work. Barbara would
tell him this was God working in his life, that this
was one of the many telltale signs that he, Carl, was
a covenant child, born to dwell in everlasting peace,
liberated forever from driving nuclear waste or milk
cross-country or even cross-county.

One of the steadily ascending high points of the walk
up Coryland Road is approaching now. Carl is on the

crest of a hill from which he can see three or four others, one rising for another few hundred feet of scrub trees and open field behind him, the others opening up half a mile or so in front of him, almost all of it planted field with intersecting copses of trees and fieldstone fences together with Beckwith Creek marking centuries-old property lines, the whole hill bisected by the long and dusty blacktop of Judson Hill Road. The Stevenson family has lived here for what seems eternity, with houses and barns Carl knows his family has had a hand in, because these houses are still known by the names of the original owners: the old Tully place, the Tuton farm, the Stevenson house. Twenty-year homeowners are still considered relatively new.

Carl's great-grandfather's name can be found on every barn in the township more than seventy-five years old. On one of the eight-by-eights, probably a center beam, about twenty feet in the air in most barns, a wood-burnt or laboriously carved *U. Stevenson*, with the year of construction. Carl wonders if Grampa Ulrich carved that name while the beam lay on the ground, or if he suspended himself somehow, with ropes or an arm, carving while he swung in the air in the smell of sawdust and cow shit. Carl likes to think he swung himself in the air to carve those letters. It is a nice picture. He imagines that he has that picture, an ancient black-and-white photo of his great-grandfather swinging in a leather harness with a chisel and hammer, a group of men watching him from the newly sawdusted floor.

As he scans the horizon he can feel his throat tightening, the green of the undergrowth now sinister and oppressive, and he quickens his pace. It's still a good two-and-a-half miles to the truck and whatever may be waiting for him there, and he's not particularly eager for the confrontation he's sure will come.

Soon he'll be passing the Jessup farm, and Carl decides to take to the woods at this point. Some feeling drives him into those trees. He doesn't want to face Jessup right now, to have to pretend to be calm and taking this all in stride, as if he knows it wasn't his fault. He hops Jessup's three tight strands of barbed wire and heads down toward the creek, planning to follow it to the end of Jessup's land and then follow the ridges and the hedgerow for the last mile or so, which will drop him off about a hundred yards downhill from Neary's farm.

The trees provide some measure of shade, though he's stirred up gnats. The creek runs a little low this year, needing the same rain that the farmers in the area need. The slate and clay of the banks are dry and cracked, with occasional small pools taken over by clouds of mosquitoes and dragonflies, who feed on the water striders riding the surface tension of the brackish water. He passes Jessup's cows, who don't notice at all, except to lift their heads and low at him occasionally. Their udders are hanging low, and Carl wonders for just a moment why Jessup hasn't milked yet.

Struggling through the undergrowth is good, Carl decides. He has not left the familiar territory of home and Myrna and work in far too long. Pulling branches aside and sinking ankle-deep into rich water grass makes him feel less nervous, less put upon by the expectations he knows the town will be putting on him.

No one can expect him to act right for a while, they will say, especially since he's responsible for it and all. Boy doesn't have much going for him, except maybe for his sister. Maybe she'll manage to pull him out of it.

They expect a certain amount of remorse, and of course Carl's sorry for the whole incident, wishes it hadn't happened, but can't see where his grief and regret become news fit for the town to traffic in. Bad news spreads. Probably Great-Grampa Ulrich Stevenson is in the middle of a barrel roll in his plot in the Judson Hill Cemetery.

He should be coming within sight of the road again, but he can't see anything but the side of the hill in front of him and a steep rise behind the creek.

After a few hundred feet he comes up on the old Boy Scout cabin, a rough, lopsided building, so he knows his sense of direction isn't gone entirely. Someone has nailed sap buckets to the maples here and never bothered picking them up, and the sidehill seems defiled, the tin rusty and the nails pulling out of the trees.

Once over the rise of the sidehill he's only a few hundred feet from the road. He can see his truck parked in front of the barn now rather than in the space next to the milk house. The house seems abandoned. He can see a tractor chugging in the long distance behind the house. A blue jay cackles in a tree nearby, apparently startled by Carl's unaccustomed presence.

It occurs to Carl again that he should stop in at St. Joseph's, or call at least, to find out if the boy's in a coma, how he's expected to do, if he's expected to live well or crippled. Barbara will probably have an update when she gets home, but Carl thinks it would probably be a nice gesture on his part to at least show some passing interest in correcting this thing he's done.

No one is nearby, so Carl gets in the truck and slips it into neutral, and it rolls back easily, though the bullet hole in the windshield is more than distracting. Carl hurries the truck in his mind, wanting to get off the Neary farm and coasting down the road to his place. As he picks up speed he sees Judith Neary come out onto the front porch, and she waves something in his direction, as if in supplication, a peace sign of some kind, but he can see her face knotted up in anger, even from this distance, and he wonders what it is she may want from him, what she thinks he may become now that he's ripped the life out of this family, but he passes over the hill and down the road and he's left with the image of Judith waving, a piece of something in her hand, wondering what she really means by it.

IN THE BLOOD

Kelly argued with his wife, Brigid, after the kids were asleep. "It's been ten years since I've seen anyone but you. I thought we agreed. Angel deserves more than a kiss-off finale."

"What are you thinking?" Brigid said. "You cannot kiss him in front of the children. Absolutely not."

"I didn't mean that and I hadn't planned on it, but now you've made me want to," he said.

"It's bad enough you waited to tell me," she said. She pulled another joint from their cubby, lit it, took a long puff, and stood there waiting for him to take it. He didn't. Finally she let out her breath and chirruped as she did. Sounded like a bullfrog.

"I wanted to wait for the former relationship question till the kids were older, and one thing led to another, and it just seemed easier to avoid it." Kelly extended his fingers. "Gimme that goddamned thing." He took a long toke.

"Now they're older, Kel, it's worse. You can't just explain bisexual to them at their age. You can try. Go ahead. I'll wait."

"They're ten and six. Hardly ancient. You know how kids are these days. They're probably already out in their circles, and we don't know it yet."

"And their dad takes it up the butt. That's a revelation. I guarantee it."

"They don't care about that." Kelly left the stub of the joint on the tea light in the center of the living room table. "You're not making this easy."

"How easy is it supposed to be? Forever and ever amen. Till death do us part? You failed on every sappy sentimental song we ever sang together in the car. Did you sing him songs?" Brigid lit another joint. The entire apartment wreathed in smoke. Just as a smoke alarm began to sound, Brigid stood on a chair and turned it off.

"No." Kelly reclined on the futon. "I didn't sing to him."

"What did you do then? Other than fuck and hike and hunt and do man things, like you say?" She stared at him, poking the joint in his direction.

"We just—hung out, carried on conversations. Just like you and I, Brigid. It's like love."

Brigid muttered, "For Christ's sake." She sat down beside Kelly. "I just don't—I can't imagine you being emotional with a man. It doesn't sit right with me."

"It's not the same, but why would it be? It's not the same relationship."

"Boy howdy, I guess not." Brigid tucked a pillow up under herself and behind and kicked him in the leg hard. "Did I not do enough? Did we not have enough sex? Jesus, is that even possible? We've fucked twice a week for the duration of our entire relationship."

Kelly sighed. "It has nothing to do with you. I love you, obviously, and I'm trying to make the family work with you."

"Is it that I'm paranoid? Because hoo, I definitely am. You're going to leave me." She stopped looking at Kelly and stood at the window, beyond which he could see the highway, suffused with fog. Route 80 would eventually lead them up old Route 15 to Mansfield, where they'd all gone to university. Brigid looked at the joint. "Did you get this stuff from Tony or Buzz?"

"Buzz, if it matters. Look, maybe you are a little paranoid."

"I think I'm more paranoid because this stuff came from Buzz. He probably soaked it in WD-40 or something. The point is you don't have a plan. You're going to go up to this man—no, don't tell me for how long, I'm not going to believe you anyway—and just calmly break contact."

"He'll be upset, but he'll understand," Kelly said. "It's been years since we argued like this. I'll stop in and tell him the same thing I told you, that I'm no longer actively bisexual."

"How do you know? What if he goes on a rampage and kills us all?"

"Please. He won't. He owns a dog. The kids are going to play with the dog, Arthur, I'm sure he's very friendly, and you and I will sit in the cabin and talk with Angel about—this."

"You make it sound easy. At least I'll be in the same room with you both. A laugh riot." She moved her foot toward his crotch.

"Please don't kick me there," he said. All in one motion she reared up on her back foot and tossed herself into his lap, kissed him hard on the mouth. Her breath smelled skunky with weed and the sweet vermouth from the martinis they'd made earlier. Brigid pushed his shirt up and his shorts down onto the futon. He raised his butt off the cushion to help her. She peeled her shirt off and smoothly disengaged herself from her bra, snapped her thumbs into the elastic of her panties, both sides, and jammed them partway down, as she had many hundreds of times before. Kelly saw the glint of tears in her eyes.

He grabbed the panties in the middle and ripped them down so he could get his mouth into her pubes. Several moments later he was inside her and she was on the verge, biting his shoulder. She looked him deeply in the eye. "I. Love. You," she said, and came down hard on his hips.

After a moment or two they gathered their clothes and hand in hand stumbled into the bedroom where they continued their lovemaking for an hour or so, hard and fast and slow and clean alternately. When they finished, he had laid one long leg over her torso. As they lay there breathing together, Kelly hit the remote to jack up the AC. Brigid said something, but he didn't catch it.

"What?" Kelly said.

In a raised voice, Brigid said, "I find it interesting that the final way you fuck me tonight is anally."

"Oh for God's sake," Kelly said.

Just then Kelly caught sight of their six-year-old son, Brandon, at the door with his PAW Patrol hat in his hand, half in and half out of his PJ bottoms.

"What's anally?" Brandon said.

* * *

"Shannon, anally is a bad word. I heard Mom say it last night and now neither Mom or Dad will talk about it." Brandon's hat was on his head now, Kelly's phone in his hands. They were on their way to Angel's in the Poconos.

"It is not a bad word. Trust me." Shannon, ten, exuded calm energy. Kelly wasn't sure how she'd gotten into this family.

"No more of this," Brigid said from the driver's seat. "We've got a long drive ahead of us. Let's not spend it arguing."

"No one's arguing," Kelly said. "Let's see how many non-Pennsylvania plates we see on the way down."

"Not again," Shannon whined. She stretched her arm toward her brother in his car seat, and, winding up, cuffed him viciously on the left ear. Brandon howled. And thus began their trip to Tannersville, Pennsylvania, the entire family pissed before they'd even left.

In the small town of Danville, they gassed up, stopping at a McDonald's to fortify themselves for the remainder of the trip. Kelly had had enough time now to think about what he would say to Angel, and he could see none of it coming out well. Angel was headstrong, and so was Brigid. Words would be thrown that couldn't be taken back, and he couldn't imagine not seeing Angel again, although for the sake of his marriage he'd try. Memories flashed in front of him: Angel's bare back shining with sweat in mid-tattooing, the diamond-shaped muscles in his calves, the way he fucked like nothing else would ever, could ever, get in the way. And it was true that he had these things with Brigid. But it just wasn't the same, and he didn't know if he was weak for not being able to overcome the differences or strong for even recognizing them. It was a difficult stone to roll uphill. And now he had a knot of cheeseburgers in the lowest part of his gut.

"What are you thinking, Kel?" Brigid said gently.

"Nothing, babe. The past. I'm letting a lot go," Kelly said. He leaned back against the headrest.

"It's for the good of the family." Brigid's firm tone belied the way she'd finished the night before after he'd gotten Brandon past the word anally. Unsuccessfully, as it had turned out. He'd sat on the bed and she'd bawled on her knees in front of him like a child, stoned and drunk. "Don't LLEEEAAAAVVVEEE me."

He tipped his ball cap down over his face. "I'm going to see if I can sleep. Feel free to change the music to whatever you want." His voice changed to something dark and charged. "Shannon, if you don't keep your hands off your brother—"

Brandon wailed.

* * *

In Swiftwater, a couple miles outside Tannersville, they stopped to make the family presentable. It was just after dinnertime. Brandon smelled like peanut butter and had the remainder of a final frozen treat smeared around his mouth. Shannon looked lost in the woods they drove through, streaming her music via huge headphones, black hair tangled like Brigid's under the headpiece. She stuck out her tongue when he reached back and poked her leg. Brigid had driven the whole way, tapping her fingers on the wheel to a music that was not playing on the Highlander's expensive sound system. They'd stopped at a McDonald's again, over Kelly's protests, Brigid wanting to keep the thing going straight and true and Kelly wanting the whole thing to be done. *Done.*

Brigid scrubbed at Brandon's lips with an alcohol wipe.

"Stop it—I don't like that. It tastes like shit." Brandon crossed his arms and kicked the back of Kelly's seat. Kelly felt the shockwaves of pain all the way up his spine.

"Brandon Lee Kerr, watch your mouth." Brigid had tied her hair back in a ponytail—they had been on the road for four hours—and had applied a spot or two of makeup.

"You're getting gussied up for Angel?" Kelly said. "You haven't done that for me in, well, ages.

139

"Someone has to keep this family on the straight and narrow."

"You can fuck right off with that talk," Kelly said. He turned his attention to the back seat. "Shannon, brush your hair." He took a brush from Brigid's purse and offered it to Shannon, who wrinkled her nose.

"Where's my brush?" Shannon said.

"I don't have your brush," Kelly said, offering it to her again, and motioning to Brigid with his eyes. Brigid had a major anger seizure working and they could all see it, her neck muscles tensing and releasing like twinned rip cords. Brandon settled back into his seat with his Godzilla plushie and Shannon ran the brush through her hair tiredly and applied lip gloss.

"OK. OK. Are we all OK now? You wanted to drive from here, right dear?" Brigid smiled. It was then Kelly noticed she'd taken off her wedding band and engagement ring. He made a mental note to talk about it later with her. He had to focus on Angel now. Kelly swallowed and hoped for the right words to come.

* * *

When they reached Angel's cabin, the weather had cooled considerably, though an abysmal heat clung to them like mist. The midges and blackflies had come out in full force. Proved what the earlier portion of the day had been like.

Angel stepped out the front door, took one look at the SUV and said, "No fun on this visit, eh? Long time no see." He didn't seem impatient. Kelly didn't know if he was feigning it, though.

"It's been a long time, and we've got to talk, Angel. But I need to introduce you to my wife and kids first."

"I know what this means," Angel said. "You can dispense with the bullshit if you want, Kelly, because that's what it is. Bullshit. You could have just emailed. I have HIV. You don't need the personal touch where it's unappreciated."

"I wanted to see you, honey, let me just explain—"

"I hope you never say that word to another man again. Because there will be other men." Behind them Brigid took matters in hand and hauled the kids out of the car. They paraded forth, and Kelly's heart sank, not for the first time. Whose terrible idea was this, pray tell? He wished he could smash a side mirror instead. Seven years of bad luck couldn't be worse than this. Angel looked much as he always had. Hair graying under his trucker cap, maybe his biceps and leg muscles weren't as pronounced. Still Angel.

"Hello, I'm Brigid. These are our kids, Shannon and Brandon. It's nice to meet you." She stopped for breath. "Angel."

"Hello, Mr. Angel," Shannon said

"Mom said you have a dog. A big one," Brandon said excitedly.

Angel sighed. "Yes, I do." He produced a worn tennis ball from the depths of his hoodie and handed it to Shannon. Angel put two fingers in his mouth and whistled sharply. An Airedale seemingly half the size of Angel's car came running and slobbering around the side of the cabin. Brandon squealed. "This is Arthur the Hippo. Throw the ball. He'll run it down for you."

It was then that Kelly noticed a gun at Angel's side, a long-barreled .44 Magnum. Basically an elephant gun. What am I in for? "Just a sec. I left something in the truck," Kelly said.

"Can we go in and sit down?" Brigid said. "I've heard your cabin is lovely." She turned beet-red. Kelly jogged back and opened the rear hatch. He grabbed his gun case and unlocked a .357 Python, popped the trigger locks and loaded it, slow as the other sins he'd committed over this ten-year period. He thrust the weapon down the back of his jeans and picked up a six-pack of Blue Moon. The farce had better look good.

* * *

"You've lived here how long?" Brigid said brightly, as Kelly and Angel sat before opened-but-untouched beers. Outside the children laughed and the dog woofed playfully along.

"Eleven years," Angel said. "Never a dull moment. If it isn't rattlers, it's bears." Angel let his eyes linger on Kelly's.

So it would be this difficult. "It's a great place," Kelly said. "There's a stream. Out back."

"Look, I know why you're here. It's copacetic. Everything is fine. You're not positive, Brigid is not positive. I am."

"You say it so calmly," Brigid said. She had noticed Angel's monster gun. "Why the gun? It's just us."

"Brigid!" Kelly spat.

"For Christ's sake, you two," Angel said, standing up, arms akimbo.

Outside Brandon screamed.

"What the fuck?" Brigid leaped to her feet and flew out the door, followed by Angel and Kelly. Outside, everyone screamed.

Hippo had torn into the left flank of a huge black bear in the gravel driveway, who sent the dog flipping and tumbling with one meaty paw, all in slow motion. Hippo slammed into the side of Angel's Suzuki, leaving a sizable dent. He gamely got to his feet to rush the bear on three paws. Angel drew his .44 and ran to within six feet of the bear's head and fired two slow shots before the bear closed on him and with both paws scattered his hat one way and his glasses another. Despite that, Angel managed another shot into the bear's massive chest before going down in a heap.

Brigid gathered the children to her by the car, pushing them inside. She started it but couldn't bring herself to leave. "What do I do?" she yelled.

"Just keep the kids away," Kelly yelled back. He sighted down his arm and put one shot, then two, into the bear's thick skull. The bear closed the distance between them. Kelly shot once more but couldn't tell if he'd hit a vulnerable spot. He thought he heard it hit flesh, then the bear was on him, teeth rending. He put his hand into the bear's mouth and shot one last time. The bear collapsed by his side, but not before stripping flesh from Kelly's arm.

Brigid ran over and helped him extricate his arm from under the bear's body. Angel came to his feet slowly, looking like a caricature of a zombie, half his face hanging off. Hippo limped slowly to Angel's side and licked his hand. Shannon and Brandon, with round O-mouths of surprise, were up against the window. Kelly felt the side of his head. He too had lost considerable flesh. Brigid had already called 911 and sirens pealed in the background. The three of them stood blindly together. Angel was inexplicably crying.

"We can work this out, Brigid." He wiped at his bloody face. "Please."

Brigid looked from Kelly to her children, finally to Angel. Kelly took Angel's hand, then Brigid's, feeling for the bare finger where her rings used to be. It wouldn't be over for a long time. If ever. Kelly squeezed Angel's hand too. Could Brigid make peace with this? Should she?

Angel took two bloody fingers and touched Brigid's face gently. "Please," Angel said through visible teeth, voice cracking like Brigid's had the night before. Brigid took out a handkerchief and tried to stroke the crimson side of his neck, and Angel shook his head, spattering blood, both bear and human, over Kelly's wounded arm and hand. By the blood, Kelly thought. God help us, we are all healed in the blood.

NUMBER A

This was not your mother's Wetonawanda. Drag Hill sat looming over the county seat like a pile of horse shit over another smaller pile of horse shit, and Johnny Piper sat in his rusted 1986 Dodge Dart in a copse of trees just off the road, waiting. Sometimes for the end of his self-appointed shift, so he could get home to his Plott hound, Willie, sometimes simply for a kind word from his wife, Dora. He didn't care that she'd been named for some famous long-dead woman the way she reminded him a couple times a week as he tried to make it with her in bed: he wanted maybe a kiss on the cheek. Romance. He wasn't a fucking machine. And she wanted Brady Bragg, drug dealer, twice-jailed hellion and raconteur.

Three weeks before, word had come down from above, the way it does, that his services were no longer required at one of his three jobs: the lightest job among them, cashier for the Dandy-Mart. With the news, Dora had packed two suitcases and her birth control pills, then hightailed it for the woods, without even a word of explanation. Her mobile phone number changed, he had no way of knowing exactly where she was, and he became, as his therapist would say, troubled.

He'd missed work, and work had missed him enough to reprimand him. Once. Then one incident at home piled over another like petty larcenies. Their daughter, Sylvia, thirteen years old and already bitter like asparagus on the tongue, might be described one way as rebellious and another way as troubled as he was. His second job, at a night-shift-only adult bookstore called Frank's Films, fired him for conduct unbecoming a retail slut. Johnny realized now that nobody knew who Frank was, but it didn't matter, just like the meth-head kids he was waiting in the trees for now didn't matter. Here, Johnny was a guy waiting for another guy—Brady Bragg—who would sell another guy drugs—meth or crack or, scary for these times, injectables like heroin—then, snorting and hopping, or cranked to the gills, Brady would drag-race his buyer down the hill and into the half-mile straight stretch before the highway and the roadside bar and restaurant, Wheaty's. Winner got a free hit, and everybody left happy, scratching themselves bloody.

Today, though, Johnny had a radar gun and a .357 Magnum (these kids could get edgy) for backup. He reported the names of the buyers he saw to State Police Officer Fritz, barracks conveniently located across from job number three, where Johnny janitored under union contract to clean the rooms where his now-missing social worker wife saved marriages and counselled lowlifes. It had been a hard but decent life, and now it was fucked. He heard the brassy gunpowder-like sound of Brady's Glasspacks coming up the other side of the hill. Brady loved the car like a pet wolf, although he also loved beating it up on dirt roads and gravelly switchbacks all over the surrounding county. Brady's love had limits, in other words, which Johnny swore deep in his heart had something to do with Dora. He knew Dora was with Brady. No limits.

Soon Brady's Frankenstein-monster Mustang came tearing down the road, a lean Trans Am not far behind, like it was 1985 again, a crescendo of exhaust fumes and whining engines passing as quickly as a John Elway rifle shot from the pocket. Johnny hit the button on the radar gun to see ninety-two on the screen. He wrote down Brady's name, put a checkmark by it, and stowed the radar gun under the seat, shoving aside a tire tool kept alongside the shifter. He looked both ways before pulling off the service road and heading toward the racers. They'd already be in the bar, and tonight he didn't feel like following them in. It would have been better if he could represent himself as a regular. No such luck. He was not a bar drinker, Johnny was a home drinker. Fuck it, he decided. One drink, and he would see Brady's face at least, and know if Dora was with him.

Inside Wheaty's the lights were low and the noise came at Johnny like a wave. A DJ high on a rickety stage spun some remixed tune with a high synthesizer part that immediately grated. As with IHOP, cafeterias, and most country bars, the '80s had never ended, but instead percolated softly in every person above a certain age, a certain swagger. Memories of the salad days. Brady and Beanie, a couple guys with full-sleeve tattoos and backward straight-brimmed hats took up two of the small tables. Brady nodded shortly in Johnny's direction. That's as much as I need, Johnny thought. He picked up his Budweiser and approached the table. Brady's right eyebrow was pierced and he had an ugly green neck tattoo.

"What up, homes?" Johnny said.

Brady tipped a bottle in his direction. "You know, this and that, a bit of the other. You know." Their eyes locked for just a moment, cracked and tinted mirrors.

"I heard your car from way outside town just now. Loud as a motherfucker," Johnny said. "Real, real loud."

"These kids all wanna make the noise," Brady said, "but they ain't got the shut up or the put up." He pointed with his bottle at Beanie, who had disappeared to the bathroom for a bump. "How you with put up, John?"

"You know me. I do all right," Johnny said.

"I see you downtown pretty regular. Like Dora says, you got a habit of coffee at Molly's?" Molly's was a tiny cafe on the same street as the police station. It had never been robbed by Brady or his type due to the regular state police presence.

"I drink good coffee, man. Wherever I find it." A look at his watch convinced him he needed to exit soon, before he accidentally said the right thing. Brady had mentioned Dora, which should have sent him into

Zone Violence, but something stopped him. Did Brady know his secret impotence? Had Dora told him?

"You one of those lazy-ass sons of bitches want a Starbucks on every corner. Vente motherfuckers got no sense. They need to keep out of shit, stick to the big cities. Elmira. Syracuse. Harrisburg," Beanie said, overhearing as he came banging through the restroom doors, rotating his head back and forth. He looked at Johnny with undisguised contempt. "Who's the bitch?" Beanie said, sneering. Before Brady could answer, Johnny abandoned his already-tense acting and stepped into Beanie's chest, who pushed him back roughly. "Oh, you're a tough guy. Three hundred pounds of shit I be kicking down the river," Beanie said.

"Fuck off," said Johnny, pushing back. Brady stepped between Beanie and Johnny before it could go any further.

"Two assholes," Brady said. "Every stupid man ends up in monkey mind, like he ain't got sense." Brady rubbed his chin.

"The fuck, Brady?" Beanie said.

"It's a Zen thing. You're trying to calm your center and here comes a dude in monkey mind, got all sorts of stuff in his brain, dunno whether to shit or go blind. You got to chill, Beanie." Brady pushed Beanie and Johnny back.

"And this fuck?" Beanie said, stepping back. "This your woman's man."

Brady held his breath for a moment, then blew it out. "He ain't nothing to stew about, Beanie. Check yourself. And Johnny. She ain't my woman. I'm just helping her."

"I was just leaving," Johnny said, shooting his cuffs as if he wore a suit. It was better to go when no one's pride had gotten too chippy. He'd have to be more careful next time. And there would be a next time. "Gentlemen," he said, and left his half-full bottle on Brady's table. Outside the darkness grew, and so did his anger.

* * *

Johnny drove home with one hand on the wheel and the other clamped on a whisky bottle he'd brought from under the seat between his legs. At every stop sign he'd take a pull, and in the forty-five minutes it took him to get home, he'd gotten pretty well toasted. All the lights were off in their modular home except the one in Sylvia's room. Willie looked like he'd trampled Dora's flowers, all dirty nose and energy.

Once inside, he yelled to Sylvia, "I'm home." Sylvia came out from her bedroom, a petite girl with hair just beginning to show roots from the black dye she normally put in it. She snapped on the light as Johnny sat down heavily, whisky slopping on the sofa.

"You seen Mom?" Sylvia said. She crossed her arms.

"Nope. She's with Brady now. I don't know when or if we'll see her." He took a pull from the bottle. "You eat yet?"

"I already had a bowl of cereal. I didn't know when you'd be home."

"Give me a minute," Brady said, squeezing the bridge of his nose. "I'll boil some hot dogs and pierogies. You need more than cereal."

"It's fine, Dad. I'm fine." A long moment passed between them, during which Johnny took another sip. Just like that, he'd gotten drunk. "Aren't you going to go get her?" Sylvia said.

"It's not that easy if she doesn't want to come," Johnny said. He stood up and weaved toward the kitchen.

"But why?" Sylvia said. "What does Brady have that you don't? I mean, I'm here too. Does she not want to see me?"

"She'll be home to see you. Right now, she can only see Brady. And what he has, darlin', is dispensable income."

"You mean disposable income?"

"Exactly." He opened the bag of pierogies and dumped it into a pot, ran water over the top.

"You're supposed to boil the water first," Sylvia said.

"This way works too," Johnny said. He put a coffee cup under the Keurig and threw in a pod of Dunkin'. Then the button wouldn't work. He sighed.

"So what are you going to do?" Sylvia sat down at the kitchen table and worried at a strand of hair. She needed a trim.

"I already did it. Went to see Brady Bragg at the bar."

"Did you beat him up?"

"No." Johnny sat down at the table across from Sylvia and laced his fingers behind his head, trying to force his mind steadier.

"Why not?"

"A lot of reasons, some of them good. If he kicks my ass, who's going to take care of you now that your mother's gone?"

"Good point. I still wish you'd tried though." Sylvia got up and stirred at the pierogies with a wooden spoon.

"I wish I'd tried too," Johnny said. "It wasn't the right time."

"So you're going to get him?" She turned to face him.

"In my own way, yep." Johnny stood up, weaving a little. "Those done yet?"

Sylvia dug the sour cream out of the refrigerator and put some pierogies in a bowl for each of them. They ate in silence, listening to the wind in the branches outside the screened kitchen window. In the distance Johnny imagined he heard the roar of Glasspacks and saw in his mind Brady Bragg laid out on the hood of his fancy Mustang like a gutted deer. The thought gave him passing satisfaction.

* * *

Johnny woke five hours after he'd gone to sleep, ready to get to his job cleaning the strip mall offices of Kings Realty, Wetonawanda Savings and Trust, and most importantly, New Wings Psychotherapy, the place Dora worked. He'd managed to make it to work these past three weeks, but she hadn't, taking a month off, according to her supervisor, under the Family and Medical Leave Act. Which left her a week to get her shit together, not that he was going to wait that long for her to make a decision between him and Brady Bragg. Needless to say, he didn't believe Brady. They were together. Johnny showered under a roaring head of steam, shaved, and laid out a banana and a packet of Quaker Oats for Sylvia for when she awoke.

The Dart started with a roar—good bones, that car had, but a Bondo body—and he pulled out of the pitted dirt driveway for the trip into town. When he got in, he pulled a ring of keys off his belt and opened the utility office, pushed the cleaning cart down the strip. Kings Realty didn't take long; he only had to pop the trash bags off their cans and vacuum the rugs, wipe down the phones and the glass front door. The Savings and Trust took somewhat longer. He needed a key and a key card both. The electronic front door locks and the loss prevention system didn't work together, and more often than occasionally he'd have to call and wake the grumbling manager to come down and reset the alarm before the state police showed up, guns drawn. Today, luckily, was not one of those days, though some fucking joker had left two leaky garbage bags on the floor that he had to haul out the back door and down the short hallway to the dumpster, then scrub the carpets.

This left New Wings. He squeegeed the front window and door first, then opened the lock and emptied the recycling and refilled the tissue boxes in each separately locked and keyed door, squirted sweet-smelling sanitizer in the bathroom pot and swirled it around with the toilet brush. Dora's office door had a poster of an Amazon rainforest. Inside, it smelled like chrysanthemums, and glossy photos of Sylvia covered a corkboard over her desk. Hang in there, a cute little monkey said, dropping by a red ribbon from the side of her ancient computer. He sighed and looked around. For a sentimental woman, she didn't show it when he came into the picture, or more accurately, the lack of pictures. He couldn't see any reflection of himself anywhere in Dora's office except in the trash he emptied and the community refrigerator he cleaned. He traced her desk blotter and came to the five days a month she affixed with a red X to denote her period. There weren't any marks for the last month. A penciled line offset the margin with two phone numbers. Johnny pulled out his phone and entered both of them as "Number A" and" Number B." He supposed that was something she must have considered before she'd FMLA'd with Brady Bragg. He locked the doors behind him.

Outside, under the overhang, he hauled a hand truck filled with six flats of soda and water. He keyed open the two soda machines at once—no one here to complain at this hour—and begin filling the slots two cans at a time until he'd finished. Finally, he'd swept the concrete frontage and emptied the two huge trash receptacles at either end and the smaller one at the sidewalk entrance. By then Betty from the bank had pulled into the back, waved to Johnny, and walked around to the front to let herself in. Johnny had finished for the morning. He pulled a warm soda from the flats stored in the utility office and sat on the concrete. It was time for his unofficial government job, watching for speeders and looking for Brady Bragg and the other small-time dealers to make a mistake.

* * *

State trooper Arnold Fritz had clued him in to the speed trap job one night after Fritz'd come in to rent *Hookers and Blow* for the third time in a month. Johnny handed him a ten and a five back from his twenty—nobody worried about change—and they'd gotten to talking, no one else in the place.

"Got a job for a guy who can keep his mouth shut," Fritz had said, toothpick hanging out of his mouth, moving up and down against his yellow teeth as he sucked at it. "Pays twenty bucks an hour, maybe twenty hours a week, varying hours. In fact, once you learn the job, you could pretty much call it any way you see fit." Johnny thought of the extra money he could make in his off hours.

"I'm listening," Johnny had said. Fritz sat with him a few times to teach him the ropes, and it wasn't as if Johnny didn't know the criminals in town already. "All right," Johnny had said to himself. "All right." And so it was. In no time he was sitting on service roads and in certain alleys, visiting the truck stop on 14 and the other adult bookstore, making note of who broke the limit and who sold the speed, all so Fritz could come in when the criminals got lazy and make the bust that would satisfy his superiors and kick him up the line into a cushier job and a better assignment. No one wanted to stay in Wetonawanda for very long.

Later that afternoon Johnny waited for Brady Bragg to come and make his daily run to Wheaty's. In the meantime, he kept alternating his thumb between Number A and Number B on his phone. Number B was a 607 area code, purchased somewhere in Elmira, New York, so he decided to try it first. He pushed the button and after a few moments a man picked up. "Brady," the man on the other end said. "Who's this?" Johnny groaned at the voice and thumbed it off. Fucking Brady.

Just in case push came to a motherfucking shove, Johnny had a five-gallon can of gas in the trunk and an old lockable Zippo lighter stashed in his pocket. Before he pushed "Number A," he brought the Zippo out and set it on the seat next to him.

Johnny managed to clock the sixteen-year-old Vanderpool kid doing a smoking 110. He put a double check next to Vanderpool. The fourth time he'd noted him this month. He'd be off the road soon via Fritz or via accident. Around four in the afternoon, just as it started getting dark, Brady Bragg came roaring through at his usual 90 miles per. No one followed him today. Brady got out of the car in the Wheaty's parking lot, and he had a woman with him. And a girl. Sonofabitch. Dora. Johnny angrily pushed "Number A." A businesslike pleasant woman answered the line. "McKinley Fertility Center," she said. "How may I help you?" Oh God.

"Can I speak with Dora Piper?" he said hesitantly.

"You just missed Ms. Piper," the woman said. "Now what was your name again?" Johnny thumbed off the line and contemplated what he had learned.

The three of them disappeared into Wheaty's. Johnny guessed they were going to eat dinner. "*Wagh*," he said aloud. Brady had taken his wife, now he would take his daughter too? Not hardly. Brady walked down the road, gas can banging against his thigh, tire tool in his off hand. He took the half-mile of road as quickly as he could. Seven or eight cars and a couple trucks remained in the driveway with Brady's Mustang. He walked over quickly and smashed in the driver's side window of Brady's ride and opened up the car. It took only seconds to douse the leather interior. Johnny backed up and threw the lit locked Zippo into the car where it exploded into a tiny poof of flame that grew larger and larger by the moment. With it, Johnny felt his hopes for a happy family grow from these ashes modestly too.

When the car had taken off sufficiently, he walked inside, the tire iron still in his hand. Dora and Sylvia and Brady sat at a back table, eating cheeseburgers and fries. Nobody at the table looked comfortable, and it took Johnny only a sad moment to realize he'd irrevocably fucked it up.

"It's not what you think." Brady looked up at him, a weary look of resignation in his eyes, then at the tire iron. "But you know that don't you? What the fuck do you want then?" Brady said.

Johnny swallowed. "Wanted to tell you," he said softly. "Your car is on fire." Just then an explosion shook the room to cries of astonishment and alarm from the patrons. Brady leapt up and rushed outside. Two or three people followed him excitedly.

"Johnny," Dora said, her eyes filling. "I wanted to have a baby. But you." She left the sentence unfinished. All around them the restaurant emptied. A swell of noise came through the door, and the smell of burning gas, an undertone of leather. The sound of sirens in the distance.

Sylvia blinked back tears too. "Oh, Daddy, that car meant the world to him." she said. "What did you do that for?"

THE POWER OF POSITIVE DRINKING

Georgette lay blissed-out in Tommy's apartment on Shirley Avenue. The cold air came in under the bedroom window and shook her out of her daydream. She'd been masturbating after Tommy left her for the shower, and as he sang tuneless songs to himself in the next room, she felt a little better about the world, less aggravated. It wasn't his fault, exactly. He seemed ignorant rather than unskilled, and as the older of the two, she'd taken it upon herself to teach him, and he was not a very good student. And so she took it upon herself to finish the job he couldn't. The heroin didn't make it any easier.

She pulled her underwear up and tucked herself into Tommy's pillow, which smelled faintly of his cologne, a scent she didn't recognize but deeply satisfied her. Tommy was a sexy kid, not too tall, but wiry, and good with his fingers, as a guitar player ought to be. She checked the bedside clock and giggled to herself. Twenty-four hours from now she would be on her way to Southern New Hampshire University. Not far from home, but far enough. Not too academically challenging, but enough. And she could still keep seeing Tommy.

And in six hours. The party.

Georgette had spent nearly all of her paycheck prepping for the going-away party. Held at Tommy's apartment, the party promised to be the social event of the early fall. All her friends from the hair salon would be there, and Tommy's friends from school, most of them home from college for the summer. She worried a little bit, though, because her cousin Ernest would be there. She couldn't think of a way to dissuade him from coming, but he promised he'd be cool as long as they kept the noise down. Cops had to have fun too.

Sheila, the owner of the Shear Beauty Salon, had helped her buy the booze. They had a full cart of liquor and a half-keg of beer, which Tommy and his roommate Charley had to haul up two flights of stairs, in the bathtub. They'd never let her forget that, she was sure. Sheila had been a bartender before she opened the salon, and she offered to mix drinks and keep an eye on people who might be drinking too much. The good news, too, was that Tommy had an extra bedroom and a large living room so people who didn't want to take the T and leave early could crash. Georgette figured on fifteen, maybe twenty people, and half of those would bail early, so there would be plenty of room. She hugged the pillow tightly. On the bedside table, Tommy had left out the cut-down straw and the dope. It tempted her, but she was still a little high. Better to wait.

* * *

Tommy soaped himself up in the shower, thinking about the sex. He'd really wanted to satisfy Georgette, but couldn't quite get her over the edge. She'd shown him what to do, where to touch her, how to say the things she needed him to say, but he couldn't quite hold out long enough. Still, Georgette, the oldest woman he'd ever been with, was also the hottest: long, straight brown hair; deep blue eyes that seemed green sometimes and other times hazel; and a set of hips that rocked his world when he had his palms on them. Some kind of fuck, in other words.

She'd introduced him to great sex, and he'd introduced her to heroin. It seemed like an even exchange. The way she'd looked the first time they'd made it together. After she'd snorted, her eyes rolled back in her head: "Jesus Christ, Tommy. Jesus Christ," and then she'd passed out. He'd awakened her after five minutes and they'd had sex for only the third time, and she'd thrust against him so hard and so fast he thought his hips would bruise. She'd exploded against him in a cloud of wetness, and he'd fallen deeply in love, immediately.

Tommy left the bathroom and went to the refrigerator. Sheila and Georgette had gone nuts with the food, hash brownies, and a couple sets of Jell-O shots, plus something Georgette called a crudités platter. Tommy still felt warm from the sex and the dope, so he decided against a beer and opened up water instead. Plenty of time for drinking later on. Charley came out of his bedroom. Six feet four and heavy, the bastard looked like an Italian gorilla, but he'd been his best friend since the sixth grade, and the only dude he'd ever claim he loved.

"What's up, punk?" Charley said.

"Nothing much. Just enjoying life." Tommy sat down on the couch.

"You left her in there alone?"

"Just for a sec. I'm thirsty." Tommy got up. "Look, I'm going back in now."

"Good man," Charley said, sitting down and turning on the TV.

* * *

Georgette guessed Tommy wasn't coming back in, but he did. She didn't give him enough credit sometimes. He tried *really hard*.

"Hi, babe," Tommy said, flopping on the bed next to her. "How was that?"

Georgette sighed inwardly. "It was really, really good, Tom."

"So…" Tommy put the water bottle on the bedside table. "Shit, I didn't realize we'd left that out." He tucked the dope and straw inside the drawer.

"That's not what I said."

"You want a drink?" Tommy said.

Georgette took the bottle from him and drank. "Can we talk about the party now?"

"Sure," Tommy said. "What do we need? We got everything in order, I thought."

"I called everybody, and most everybody confirmed. That's awesome, yeah?" Georgette didn't think Tommy had invested himself as heavily in this party as she had. He hosted it sure, but didn't seem as excited as he ought to be.

"Yeah. This is the last hurrah, you know?" He tucked her hair behind her ear. Always trying.

"Oh, baby. I'm only going to be an hour away."

"That's different from being right here. I mean—"

"You're sweet, but I'll be home every weekend." Georgette planned on coming home, sure, but she didn't plan on it every weekend. A little white lie wouldn't hurt though. He needed to hear it.

"I know," Tommy said. "It's just I'll get distracted. I'll miss it." Georgette could feel her high slipping away.

"You know what I miss," she said, and pulled at his jeans. Rolling over top of Tommy, she fiddled his zipper open. Even as she went down on him, she thought about the drawer.

* * *

Since he'd started Charley running, the man had dropped fifteen pounds, and Tommy himself liked the way running felt, how he could feel his heartbeat high in his chest. Running along the beach up to Point of Pines and back down into Winthrop would be just right. Nothing huge, no ten-miler or anything, just something to kick the sex off his bones. Georgette had left to find Sheila and get her hair done before the party. He guessed he should take it more seriously. A pang hit him in the gut, and he stopped and reached for his toes, trying to stretch it out of his body like he did when they ran. Lately, since he started jogging with Charley, he'd gotten better at working bad thoughts out of his body like a cramp.

"Let's go, slowpoke. All that fucking has messed with your brain." Charley jogged in place, tiny biker shorts on his big body looking a little odd. They ran past the Revere Beach T stop, where a swarm of late-season beachgoers came and went. To their right on the side of the pavilions was a group of brown-skinned men and a couple women in modest suits playing volleyball. As they ran, they dodged passersby frequently, but kept a modest pace here where the crowds were thickest. Approaching the Point, people would thin out and they could pick up the pace.

"My brain is just fine," Tommy said, breathing easily.

"Says you," Charley said. "Bike coming!" They swerved out of the way of a bicyclist. "Fuck off," they heard as the man went by in a swoosh.

"Asshole," Tommy said.

"So you think Georgette can hook me up with Sheila?" Charley said, puffing. They took the left side of the street and ran past Figaro's, closed for the day as usual.

"No shit? Sheila?" He knew Charley wanted Georgette, so this came as a little bit of a shock. What was he up to?

"You know. You had some luck with an older woman, I figured maybe I can, too." Charley jogged with his elbows high, still slightly uncomfortable in his own body. Tommy laughed. "You think you can handle an older woman?"

"She's not that old. And I can handle anything you can. Bet your ass," Charley said.

* * *

At the salon, Sheila sat Georgette in a chair and fiddled with her hair. "So what do you want me to do, chick? You want me to do some quick highlights? You want a trim?"

"Actually, I want a big change. Dye me auburn."

"Really?" Sheila paused and flipped her hand to the side. "Though your hair will take auburn pretty readily. If you want it, I'm game."

"Right!" Georgette relaxed in the long chair. Sheila would take care of her just fine.

"So this is a big deal," Sheila said. "Going off to college. It's what you've been saving for."

"I think so." Georgette closed her eyes, trying to will back her sudden panic. It was what she'd been saving for, but she'd be leaving so much behind: Sheila, Tommy, comforts of home. "Can we talk about something else?"

"How about the fact that your boyfriend's roommate has the hots for you?" Sheila said.

"Oh God. Don't remind me."

"I mean, the poor kid is not unattractive."

"In a gorilla way. Hairy and huge and Italian. If you like them like that."

"You have a nice-sized boy. Tommy is very nice," Shei-

165

la paused and took her gloves off. "You're set for now. I'll be right back. Gotta pee."

Georgette tried to relax, but the more she'd tried to enjoy the sensation of being taken care of, the more her eventual departure weighed on her. She'd come down, for sure. But she'd be leaving it all behind. But Tommy would still be there.

"So, what are you going to do about Charley?" Sheila said after she'd returned. After a moment, Georgette considered.

"I don't know. I think the problem will take care of itself. Out of sight, out of mind."

Georgette folded her hands in her lap, surprised to find her fingers were trembling.

"It'll pass. You could have worse problems."

"Ugh," Georgette said. "I could, at that."

*　*　*

Tommy waited at the apartment. Both he and Charley had showered after their run and cleaned up: dumped the garbage, put the dirty clothes into closets, cleaned out the fridge, made a half-hearted pass over the bathroom toilet, tapped the keg. Tommy put the baked goods out on the table, and whatever that platter was.

Between the two of them, they managed to hang the "Congratulations!" banner, then Tommy went to the bedroom next and made up the bed, figuring he and Georgette wouldn't be the only ones sleeping there tonight. He wasn't expecting a puppy pile, but he was the host and felt responsible for people having a good time and a place to sleep one off. By 6:30, Georgette's friends had begun showing up. Charley answered the door first, greeting two blonde women with an expansive wave of his hand. *"Mi casa su casa,"* he said, and Tommy groaned. He appraised the women carefully. Maybe one of them would go for the gorilla.

* * *

Sheila and Georgette got out of Sheila's car tottering on their low heels, having stopped off for a couple shots at the Shipwreck Lounge before returning to Tommy's. "Priming the pump," Sheila said. Georgette heard the music as soon as she got out of the car and checked her watch. Yikes. It was nearly 7:40. Tommy would be pissed. She hoped he liked her hair. She caught sight of herself reflected in the car window: slim woman, big hips, long auburn hair now, dark sunglasses. Hot, in a word.

"Sounds like they got started without us," Georgette said.

"Party doesn't start until we get there," Sheila said. Sheila looked fine, too, her short hair done up and spiked to the side like a punk rocker. She had the cheekbones to pull off that short hair, and knew how to highlight them. It would be a good night.

Georgette held Sheila's hand as they walked up the steep steps. One short flight to the landing, then the two flights to Tommy's apartment where the bass was banging the walls. Good thing it was mostly immigrants and young people living here. One wouldn't complain, and the other couldn't, really. She hoped Ernest wouldn't show up. Having a cop in the place would be a real downer, even though he'd assured her things would be cool.

Tommy opened the door before she'd even approached it. Behind him, she could see Jill and Angela, some friends from the gym, and a few of Tommy and Charley's friends she didn't know terribly well, all sitting on the couch or talking leaning against the walls, maybe ten people total. Tommy kissed Georgette, then Sheila, on the cheek, then led Georgette by the hand into the apartment. "Woo-hoo!" he yelled over the hip-hop, and everybody laughed and began clapping. Georgette began to relax a little. Across the room, Charley smiled at her and saluted with his red Solo cup.

* * *

Tommy whispered in her hair. "I like it a lot."

Georgette smiled at him. "I just thought it would be cool. New start and all." Tommy kissed her ear, but he didn't like the sound of that. New start. Away from him. Not good. He shook himself like a bear.

"You okay?" Georgette asked. He nodded. "Sweet Tommy," she said.

"Just a chill," he said. Charley had brought her a screwdriver already, and Georgette was half into it in about ten minutes, the music blaring louder now, the apartment filled with people they both had to greet. Tommy followed her around, meeting all her friends and smiling, leaving only to get them both drinks. Charley shouldn't have an issue in a room full of hot women. In the bathroom, he found the keg sideways already, the tap angled out into the room rather than parallel to the walls. Tommy lifted it back into place and threw his back out of whack a bit. Georgette looked good as a redhead, he had to admit. He wondered what it would be like later in bed, running his hands through it.

Back outside, the party was in full swing. Georgette stood in the corner of the kitchen talking with Charley and Sheila. Charley had his hand rested on the wall right next to Georgette's face and was leaning in close to talk with her, his face conspiratorial and buried in her red hair, while Sheila just laughed. He watched as Georgette took another drink from her cup and stared into it, giggling. Charley took it from her and went to the drink table, mixing up another screwdriver, heavy on the vodka, and Tommy took all this in as if it were happening somewhere else to somebody else. He dissociated from all the noise momentarily and thought about running the beach with Charley.

Just then, his friend Marco corralled him by the arms and took him out on the fire escape to smoke a bone. At least Sheila was there, mixing drinks for other partygoers. She wouldn't let anything happen. And Ernest, her cop cousin, stood by the TV, looking out of place. She was leaving anyway, he caught himself thinking.

*　*　*

Georgette saw Tommy leave with Marco. She didn't feel buzzed yet. She didn't know if Tommy had told Charley to lighten the drink so she wouldn't get drunk, or what, but she was determined to make this party work. She excused herself to the bedroom. It wasn't as if she hadn't been thinking about it all night, just getting back to that nice mellow feeling, that rich high, the one thing she shared with Tommy, sweet Tommy, and no one else. She closed the door behind her and went to the bedside table and cut out three fat lines. One for each nostril and one to grow on. She pulled out the straw and took in one line and paused. Then the heat took over and she fell backward onto the bed, bouncing off, then hitting the floor.

* * *

Charley stood in the doorway of the kitchen talking with Sheila, who looked fine in her tight skirt, like that singer from the '80s with the funky short hair. Couldn't remember her name. But fine. And she actually talked with him, asking about his job at the YMCA and what he planned to do with the rest of his life. He felt like he was finally getting somewhere with this woman. Since he'd spent most of the summer with his dick in his hand thinking about his roommate's girlfriend, it was a welcome change.

"Hey," Sheila was saying something he couldn't quite hear. He had to bend down closer to her mouth, as the party had taken another turn with the latecomers finally having made an entrance. "Have you seen Georgette?" Sheila yelled.

"Not in a while," Charley said. "Maybe she and Tommy, you know, hit the bedroom. The door is closed. I'll go check."

"I'll go with," Sheila said, taking him by the hand. Charley flushed all over.

170

He knocked on the door first softly, then harder. No answer. He opened the door slowly, with Sheila right beside him, and they saw Georgette sprawled on the floor.

"Holy fuck," Charley whispered. Sheila rushed past him and knelt down, slapping Georgette around the cheeks.

"Wake up, honey," Sheila pleaded. "For Christ's sake, wake up. Oh fuck. Go get Tommy."

Charley pulled Tommy in, and he sat there numb, trying to make sense of it all. Charley was on his cell phone, then shut it off. Tommy grabbed her by her new auburn hair and pulled at it. Her head rolled-loosely.

"We've got to be practical," Charley was saying to no one in particular. "We've got to get her out of here." Georgette's cousin, the cop, tried CPR, but her lips were already blue. Tommy backed out of the room, taking a big swig from Charley's red cup, almost re-lieved that she looked so different, like someone else, someone long gone, and he wouldn't have to bother with saying goodbye.

ABOUT RUSTY BARNES

Rusty Barnes is author of the story collections *Breaking it Down* (sunnyoutside, 2007), *Mostly Redneck* (sunnyoutside, 2011), and *Kraj: The Enforcer* (Shotgun Honey, 2019), as well as four novels: *Reckoning* (sunnyoutside, 2014), *Ridgerunner* (Shotgun Honey, 2017), *Knuckledragger* (Shotgun Honey, 2017), and *The Last Danger* (Shotgun Honey, 2018). His fiction, poetry, and nonfiction have appeared or are forthcoming in many journals and anthologies like *Dirty Boulevard: Crime Stories Inspired by the Songs of Lou Reed* (Down & Out Books, 2018), *Best Small Fictions 2015*, *Switchblade*, *Mystery Tribune*, *Goliad Review*, *SmokeLong Quarterly*, *Red Rock Review*, *Porter Gulch Review*, and *Post Road*. His poetry collections include *On Broad Sound* (Nixes Mates Press, 2016) and *Jesus in the Ghost Room* (Nixes Mates Press, 2017). He founded and edits *Tough*, a journal of crime fiction and occasional review. He lives in Revere, Massachusetts, but grew up in rural northern Appalachia. You can find him on X @rustybarnes23.